WOLFGANG

BOOK 1

BEWARE OF THE DOG

WILL LORIMER

This book is a work of fiction. Names, characters, businesses, organisations, places, events, and incidents are imaginary. Any resemblance to actual persons, living or dead, or locales, is entirely coincidental.

ISBN (print) 978-1-8381382-4-0

INKISTAN
.COM

THE NEW LAIRD'S OLD CLOTHES

Za-Za was seated at her typing station, holding a small antique hand mirror up to her right eye, when Wolfgang flounced into the sparsely furnished Victorian conservatory and slammed the pantry door behind him.

Stealing a glance in her direction, he gathered his tartan dressing gown more securely about his flanks and slipped into a highbacked Indian cane chair, strategically positioned to avoid drips from a cracked pane above. With a sigh, he stretched out, propped his paws up on the pine sill, and silently regarded his embroidered Arabian leather slippers, the only pair he had left after his wife had donated the rest to a charity shop in the nearby town. They'd been snapped up by a collector, he'd later heard.

Formerly the pride of his collection, the slippers looked ridiculous to him now, with their fluffy red pom-poms. He couldn't imagine why he had them specially made, far less paid the exorbitant price of the oily Oriental who had measured his paws, down on his hands and knees on a worn old rug, in the slipper souk of a dusty bazaar somewhere in the Middle East. That was on one of his trips with Brünhilda. Istanbul? Or maybe Marrakesh – though that was to the south. Africa? Never mind. The great advantage of travelling with the Duchess was that, having a pigeon brain, she never got lost. Any shit going on passed her by, and trouble missed altogether, like she was protected by an invisible sheath. But the downside was, of course, he always drew the fire.

Aristocrats, can't put up with 'em, best without, he thought. *Accept it, she's gone, gone, into an abyss of her own choosing.* As surely as if she had been sucked into the plug hole of the cast-iron monstrosity with the lion's feet in the west turret bathroom, next to their bedroom in the eves, leaving only per-fumed suds and a slick of Allure №.5 in the bath which was thoroughly impregnated with her expensive scents already.

Changing his perspective, he looked, via the vagaries of Victorian glass, towards a faint line of treetops blotted by low cloud, behind the blur of the siege wall. Veiled by drifting rain, it seemed far off but was a bare 150 yards distant. Appropriately, the wall, which was high but not unscalable, had proper abutments in keeping with the castellated buildings of the dimin-ished estate, and had been built to specifications laid down by Harold of that Ilk, the 13th Laird of Castle Haggard, her great-great grandpapa, who had to sell off 500 acres of good arable land and 2 hill farms to pay for it. Designed to impress distinguished visitors to the castle's famous maze, its principal purpose, however, was to keep the revolting peasantry out of the large vegetable garden during the hungry years of the 30's, when Castle Haggard was defended by local militia. But then the garden and its tricky maze designed to trap intruders came under sustained attack, and the old laird was forced to order a tactical retreat.

The historic episode was recounted in the Haggard Year Book of '33. In Volume III of that year, he'd found a sepia photograph taken after the siege was lifted, showing trenches crossing the garden and its famous fork-ing paths heaped with soil. Faded articles in newspapers of the day praised the defenders, and an editorial in the Kingdom Times cited it as an example of the not-insignificant part such minor actions played in turning the tide of the Great Civil War.

In one photograph, estate workers toasted the Laird as he stood up on the steps to the great hall, holding the blunderbuss with which, it was re-ported, he had shot one of the assailants in the leg. The celebrations how-ever had been short-lived. All too soon, the spoils of victory arrived. Credit dried up, government war bonds became worthless. Banks closed their doors against angry depositors. Money stopped circulating, the economy crashed, factories closed, bankruptcies soared. Dole queues disappeared down manholes around street corners. In the countryside, the great estates of the gentry fell into disrepair. Some unfortunate aristocrats even had to sell land –The 13th Laird being no exception, and Haggard Hill was lost in the 'Great Estate Sell-off', as the Snaresburgh Dispatch reported at the time.

Long decline followed, the vegetable garden and its famous maze was lost to weeds. Then Brünhilda was born, her late arrival seen by locals as something of a minor miracle, because her mother was 52, and it was known the Laird and Lady of the castle rarely talked, and their bedrooms were in the east and west wings, respectively. Though not exactly an idyllic situation for a young child, at least she had Nanny to look after her in the big house, and there was lots to explore. Her bestest hiding place was the rusty clock room under the eves of the Castle Tower, where she would sweep the boards clear of beetles' droppings, spread out sacking, lie down and stare up at the patch of sky exposed in a gap in the slates of the Clock Tower roof. Her favourite dreams were of spinning wool, weaving tapestries on a loom in that room, of entertaining friends she hadn't met yet who would admire the bright colours of her tapestries, and of having mad parties in the great hall, after she inherited the castle.

But when Brünhilda turned 13, her father, in despair at the quarry blasting away the granite crag of the original castle on Haggard Hill, and the predations of death watch beetles in the tower, left the ancestors' portraits to rot in the great hall, boarded up the big house and rented a bungalow from a former tenant on the facing hill, having leased the castle and stables to a pig farmer, much to the displeasure of his daughter and only heir.

Ten years later, the old laird died of apoplexy. It was widely supposed the attack was brought on because he hated living in the bungalow. However, there were doubts. Some thought it was to do with the 10-year lease of the pig farmer being up, and the prospect of having to move back into the big house. Others, perhaps more perceptive, thought it was the laird's shock at reading in the Dispatch that plans for the great Snaresburgh bypass had been shelved and Castle Haggard would not now be demolished. Further weight was added to their speculations, because that day's edition of the Snaresburgh Dispatch had been found beside his cold dead body, lying open on the front page under the headline, *CASTLE HAGGARD SAVED*. But whether relief or disappointment, that surely was the final blow.

But no one spoke about that at the glorious June wedding, when the sun shone on bride and groom, and there was a great party after, with a band who later became famous with several No.1 hits. Hash cakes got mixed in with the hors d'oeuvres and served to one and all. It was all very democratic. Distinguished guests, among the common crowd of friends and former estate workers, never suspected. It was great fun, everyone agreed.

The newly married couple had only been in the big house a week when Wolfgang blew up the granite pig sties in the great hall, starting his renovations with a bang. To celebrate they popped bottles of bubbly and got rather tipsy with the quarry man, who had provided the TNT sticks, detonators and expertise for twenty quid on the QT. A price, he declared with a wink, which would have been downright insulting if blowing up the castle hadn't been his dream since hearing about the siege from his grandfather, who limped from buck-shot he took in the leg from the old laird's blunderbuss.

Inspired by the progress Wolfgang was soon making with hired men press-ganged from the pubs in nearby Snaresburgh, Brünhilda's merry band of women helpers, aided by the ever-willing but hapless Cockroach, soon set to in the vegetable garden. The Sisters of the Soil, as the feminist collective called themselves, toiled long hours to restore the garden to its 19th century salad days. Beds were raised according to modern methods, but on Brünhilda's insistence castle traditions were maintained. All agreed the box hedges lining the maze of pink gravel paths looked much the same, when compared to old photographs in the Haggard Year book of 1899. The photos had been taken by a Count Kinsky from Bohemia who had stayed at the castle with his wife, Countess Constanze, a Georgian Princess. Later, she'd privately published a monogram published about their tour of the great gardens of the Kingdom. Special mention was made of their promenade in Castle Haggards's famous garden of forking paths. A sepia photograph showed the distinguished couple surveying the regimented legumes, divisions of carrots, onions and artichokes – Jerusalem and globe – the neat net fruit cages, the paved areas with alpine flora under glass, the cress beds in the corner of the garden where a little steam entered by a culvert under the siege wall.

However, once again, the vegetable garden and its famous maze of forking paths had fallen into ruination. The organic beds which over three summers the weekend lesbians had sifted, riddled, and dug with such care, not to mention increasing the fertility of the soil by sprinkling their menses, sadly were now overgrown with a riot of brassicas and Jerusalem artichokes, bamboo cane thickets, clumps of shooting spinach. Here and there, great heads of poisonous hogweed hovered above swaying stands of pampas grass, which had gone to seed since Brünhilda had left.

Though testament to her green fingers, and perhaps the power of lesbian menses too, still it was disturbing how much the plants had grown since, given it was barely two months, he considered, spying a blackened brassica like a monstrous Olmec head lurking under some jungle fronds. No doubt it was one of Brünhilda's exhibition cabbages, which had turned rotten in her absence. With its black eye patch of mould and split skin grin, it resembled more a giant skull than a blotched and decaying white Dutch cabbage.

A goddamn skull! he realised with a stab of paranoia, *Skull was Dutch, wasn't he?*

'And what is the matter with a singularly dishevelled laird this late morning?' Za-Za demanded, laying her mirror down on a fresh ream of paper by the old fashioned Imperitor typewriter, once owned by a countess, swivelling her chair to get a better view on his averted face.

'Bloody weather, I hate it!' Wolfgang replied, brushing back a lick of thick black hair that had fallen across his unshaven cheek. He'd first noticed it was shot with stray silver strands three days after Brünhilda split from the castle in his pre-war Lamborghini of the long running boards - disappearing in a haze of blue exhaust smoke, because she could never work the clutch of HIS CAR, leaving him her rusting vintage Riley. It was also inherited from her beloved papa, which, like the old Laird had, spluttered a lot and regularly broke down.

'Come-on, spit it out! I'm not starting work with you in this foul mood.'

'The book, the castle.' He twisted round, actually *looked* at the gorgon for the first time that day - he had to, so better sooner than later. 'I hate it all, and that's not to mention my absconding wife.'

'And what's brought this on?'

'After everything we've been through, you ask me that?'

Tossing back her tawny mane, she exposed an ivory, surprisingly muscled throat - the muscles no doubt from all the blowjobs she gave Skull, he thought darkly. Then Za-Za rolled a laugh over Verushka pin-up shoulders, and what Wolfgang considered to be perfect Popocatepetl nipples peeked up through the uncertain mists of a discoloured T-shirt two sizes too big for her, a shirt that said 'Wannabe a Rock Legend', in cluster fucks of faded blue stars over an apocalypse wasteland, LA or somewhere, zombies of the hood skulking in doorways at dusk.

'I know just because of last night ...' She blinked at him.

'As if I cared about your lover...' *Bitch,* he thought, wondering if she'd gotten the T-shirt from Skull. Looked to be about his brute size. *Fuck him.*

'Former lover…'

Wolfgang shook his head, stood up and, edging past her wingback swivel chair, gave it and its occupant a twirl.

Then he laughed. 'Sure didn't look that way when I found you both in a clinch at the back of the bar.' Happier now, he loped across the conservatory's red stone tiles toward the stove in the corner. Reaching the log basket, he stooped, looked round, and half-snarled, 'Anyway, I thought you hated Skull. What was that about?'

'I have to keep him sweet,' Za-Za said, staring up at thickening clouds through cracked panes, continuing to swivel idly back and forth in the chair, her arms dangling over the wingback. 'He can be very dangerous you know …'

'I don't doubt that.' Wolfgang cast a handful of chaff on the embers, fed in twigs, puffed up flames, put on two logs, closed the rusty iron door of the old pot belly stove with a clang. He padded back to her chair. 'How don't you ever get cold?' he asked, looking down at her.

'It doesn't bother me. See?' Staring back up, she pinched her chubby cheek. 'This kitty has a thermal layer of subcutaneous fat all over. It's unique to Inuit cat genes, skin that doesn't wear out. I'll never get wrinkles.'

'Even kitty Inuits from the good ol' USA get wrinkles in their forties. It's a proven fact,' he said, affecting what he imagined was a Kentucky drawl.

'I won't live that long.'

'Scary.' Wolfgang turned his Indian cane chair around to face her, sat down, and folded his hands in his lap.

'Crash and burn, that's me, baby."

'What about Skull?' he asked.

'Nemo me impune laessit, that's him.'

'What's that mean?'

'*No one insults me with impunity.* Boy, that Skull holds a grudge like no other.'

'Oh great. Just what I need with his background in the Special Forces.' Wolfgang frowned, crossed his arms, gathered his dressing gown more tightly about his flanks. 'Or so you say.' He arched a quizzical eyebrow. 'You did tell him you're only my secretary?'

'Yes, but he doesn't believe me.'

'Show him your employment contract then. It's a legal document. That should convince him, surely?'

'I did, and he tore it into little pieces. He was particularly angry about the porridge.'

'What? That contract had to be drawn up at short notice. Jaws doesn't come cheap you know, for all I keep him on a retainer.'

'Your wife must be very rich to be bankrolling all this.' Za-za said, raised a broad hand (which would have looked outsize on a transvestite brickie) towards the dripping black stones of the castle's clock tower, which loomed over the conservatory.

'Unfortunately that well dried up some time ago.' He shook his head. 'She's got her own lawyers now. Smiggle, Pagan and Thorpe. Fortunately Jaws went to school with Simon *goofy* Armitage.' Wolfgang crossed his eyes and made a Bugs Bunny face. 'One of the partners. Jaws is hopeful they can work something out under the desk, so to speak.'

'The old school tie brigade huh?' Za-Za's blue eyes twinkled like brilliant sapphires, set in Fabergé eggs formed of Siberian snow. In the icy distance across the tundra, a wolf howled.

'Yes, and a bloody good thing too as far as I'm concerned.' Wolfgang grinned hugely, thinking, *Great cheekbones too. Just what the doctor ordered after SHE packed up and left. All I need now is an early fall of snow, arriving on an anticyclone from Norway, to provide the excuse to harness up the old Muscovite*

sleigh, gathering dust half a century or more in the stables, and then get out Great-
great Grandmama's sable from the box in the No.2 store, from that count she met
before the revolution... snuggle up and see what occurs ....

'So how come you and Brünhilda ever got together?' She asked, harshly, as if divining his last thought, arching an eyebrow over the tortoiseshell-backed hand mirror with the castle crest inlaid in silver, which she'd filched from Brünhilda's dressing room, earlier. 'You're not exactly in the same league, are you?'

'No.' frowning, he shook his head, wondering where he had seen the mirror before. 'Much as he would have loved to board me out, my Oxbridge educated ex-army officer *father* would never have countenanced shelling out for school fees as his father did. Instead, I was sent to a failing state com-prehensive where I was ridiculed for my wolf legs.'

He let out a sigh, reflexively stroking woolly flanks wrapped in the tartan of his clan, the McNemos – a broad check, brown and yellow squares, on a green background, crossed by thin red bands – which Brünhilda had woven on her loom, now abandoned in her weaving studio in the clock room of the east tower.

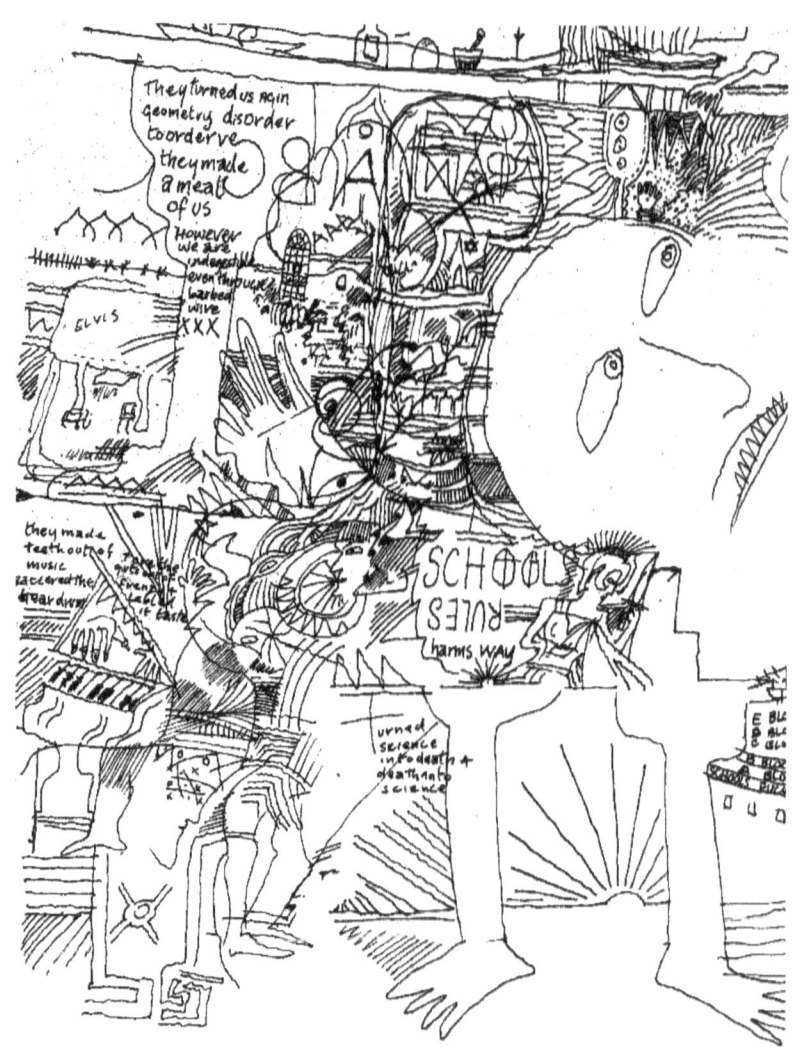

'It was a horrible school,' he went on, 'From day one, I was made to wear excruciating special shoes to shape my paws into *proper* feet. Then, not withstanding my high IQ, I was demoted to the remedial class when my step-mother insisted, in another of her good deeds' – an ironical chuckle – 'presenting the school with a wire mesh cage to keep me in, even though I had only been defending myself.' Wolfgang paused, realizing he had been panting. 'Where was I?'

'Brünhilda,' Za-Za said, dryly.

'Oh yes, the Duchess.' Wolfgang winced. Pretending, he probed a finger at a tooth, covering the slip. 'You know how it is with aristos.' He shrugged as if that explained everything.

'You forget I was born in a gulag in the old Soviet Union and brought up in the decadent USA. I find the class system in this mouldering Kingdom completely baffling.'

'Blue-blooded aristos such as my beloved wife, with their eccentricities of breeding and bifurcating lineages are born peculiar. Different from plebeians as, say, anthracite is from common coal. Conditioned from birth by wet nurses, nannies, and the parental neglect that comes with the territory, before being packed off to boarding school, aged seven, jolly hugs and goodbyes, suitcases on the platform. Date of birth, destination and return address, on a label tied to the button of said child's blazer. Onto the steam train, this being the Kingdom, placed in the guard's van, until they're collected from the station of destination by special arrangement. Or, if parents are sentimental, in the Rolls with James the chauffeur chain smoking the long drive to the other end of the country.

'Either way, before they know it, they are conjugating Latin verbs, cribbing and undergoing medical inspections by day, if lucky having g the occasional injection in the buttocks from Matron. At night, mutual masturbation in the dorms, when not sore from black-balling by prefects, or too bloated from midnight feasts. Monday afternoons Army, Navy and Airforce cadets, marching in the playing fields, standing to attention and presenting arms. Tuesdays, Thursdays, and Saturdays, jolly hockey sticks, and inter-school cricket matches to endure, acne blistering in the summer sun. In winter, rugby in the mud, in opposing packs called scrums, pushing their heads against the other forwards' bottoms, while their teammates look on, before the referee blows his whistle and they do it again.

'Sunday at Chapel the good lord is our form master who canes us, we shall not want and God save the old alma mater. But even after all this, still no escape for the aristos, yet more humiliation.' Wolfgang looked up, checking she was listening.

'The girls of course,' he continued, 'on to Swiss finishing schools in the Alps, and lady lessons in deportment, dinner table etiquette, macramé and bedroom manners, before passing out to a season of deb balls, after which, endowed with a dowry and the hand of a landed scion, blessed with good pedigree hopefully. Meanwhile, the boys onwards and upwards to Sand-hurst and the Army, forced marches on the Brecon Beacons, forwards to the frontiers of Afghanistan, in command of a platoon of real men, after-wards to write a book about it. Then a job in the City with Daddy's stock-brokers. Or better still, brain transplants in cloistered halls, where dons in gowns cram their already swollen cerebrums with dead languages, useless theories and undigestible facts. Yes Oxbridge, where they join pig fucking fraternities that tie them for life, when not hunting and shooting on their estates, pontificating in the House of Lords, serving as MPs, taking consul-tancies, company directorships, and otherwise contributing to society.

'Bred for leadership,' Wolfgang continued, addressing an imaginary au-dience in the stalls and grand circle, looking back adoringly through pince-nez and opera glasses, instead of just a disengaged secretary filing her nails, placidly. 'Met everywhere with deference, but sneered at upon departure, consumed by feelings of worthlessness and shame all their lives, crushed by privilege, the final form of Homo Reflugent Patricus which, if you recall, began its remarkable journey in life as exotic coal, is refined carbonite, facetted with sharp edges that need smoothed off if they want to bob along with the flotsam – the rest of us, washing in and out in the mucky tide, on the beach of human affairs.

'I'm relatively speaking the rough, as in uncut, diamond, delivered by a wave that raked the shingle rather more deeply than the preceding forty-eight, that's all. It's an age-old story. I'd been sleeping in sand a thousand years. Time to wake up. She just got lucky when I crashed her coming out ball.' Wolfgang laughed.

'Oh so that's how it happened.' Za-Za yawned, replaced her nail file in its case, and reached for the mirror again.

'Yes.' Wolfgang sat down suddenly, remembering his first sight of Brünhilda, shimmering in a sequined, body-hugging green dress. 'It was love at first sight. She the moth and I the flame. Or the other way round? The feeling was *mothtual*. Yes, it was. Don't look like that at me,' he glared, 'it's a real word. All the chinless wonders in the ballroom just couldn't compete. I was Romeo in a bolero hat still dripping from the forty-ninth wave, a scarlet sash to go with a high-waisted matador's jacket with epaulettes and red sequins that complimented hers. Tights and pumps to match. We fandangoed, becoming hot, I soon dried off, all the time her father watching, disapproving.

'We made a swift exit by the stage door, ended up in the park nearby, drinking champagne, and making out on a pink drift of May blossom falling like snow from the cherry trees around, and howling up at a sickle moon.'

'Tell me, was it waxing, or waning?'

'Why d'you ask?'

'Just curious. I'm interested in how the workings of fate coincide with the phases of the moon.'

'Waxing I think.' He paused, uncertain. Absently, he stroked his three-day stubble. 'Yes, definitely.'

'So what went wrong, Wolfie?' Za-Za asked, laying the hand mirror back down on the table.

'Za-za,' Wolfgang exclaimed, suddenly noticing the purple swelling above his secretary's right eye, 'what's that bump below your eyebrow?'

'Oh, just an embolism.' She shrugged. 'A little closer to my brain and I might be dead. Too much spike and not enough sleep these past months, I guess.' She grinned, producing a glass vial of grey powder from her waist pouch. 'Fancy a couple of fat lines to get the creative juices going, Wolfie dear?'

'This spike is fucking A!' Wolfgang, who had recently developed quite a taste for the designer drug, raised his head from the mirror. 'Where did you get it?' he said, distracted by his nose which, dusted by powder, looked distinctly luminous reflected in the conservatory's mildewed glass, as the afternoon light of that already crepuscular day dimmed outside.

'I told you I had to keep Skull sweet.'

'Oh no, not him.'

'Yes, Wolfie, and he's promised me more later. It's the best, all the way from Chetznia in the diplomatic bag.'

'The diplomatic bag, really?

'Silly Wolfie,' she tutted, 'that's just the way, not the means.'

'Of course,' he nodded, not sure he quite understood.

'Now, are you going to get down to work? Your choice, it's nothing to me, as long as I get paid.'

'Uh, yea, but can I have another line please? You know how it is.' He angled his hand above his eyes. 'Not quite reached the altiplano yet. I *can* see the high plateau, but, you know...' He pleaded.

'I'll need extra porridge.'

'Of course, that's a given, Za-Za. I'll top you up with the special golden oaties later. No problem. Always plenty more porridge at Castle Haggard.' He grinned wolfishly, his mind already on his composition of the day.

At her station Za-Za ratcheted the wheel of the old typewriter, feeding in a sheet of blank paper under the watchful gaze of the double-headed eagle of Imperitor typewriters, manufactured in Budapest, circa 1890. However, in 1913 the company went bust, owing to litigation over spelli g errors in the 9th draft of the Treaty of Veristipol between the Austro-Hungarian Empire and the Ottoman Empire, which so enraged Gervilo Pincip, a Serbian literalist of the Black Hand Order, that he shot Arch-Duke Franz Ferdinand and triggered World War I. The trademark emblem of the infamous Tripewriter Corp. (and the Austro-Hungarian Empire), so dominant in the early 20th century, and played such a big role in the fall of the great European empires, stood with its gilt wings spread, its golden claws securely annealed to the top bar of the typewriter, the imperial double head well above the complications of characters and symbols, of misaligned and bent keys within the mechanism's scratched black metal casing.

PROPHESY'S END

Archangel, June 23rd by the light of the midnight Sun.

Wolfgang is dead. Sadly, not the vainglorious death he would have awarded himself, immolated in his renovated castle like a Viking lord. Instead it was a miserable end, weeping for a clutch of emeralds he'd swallowed in a last desperate bid to thwart his assailants. They'd tracked him down to his seedy hotel room overlooking a meat market in Bogota. But before he died, he did manage to pen a last few words in his notebook – which I am pledged never to divulge – addressed to Brünhilda, his estranged wife, the obsessional subject of so much of his writings. Persistent to the end, as befits a laird of his McNemo cloth, he also wrote to the Kingdom Consul in Colombia instructing the diplomat to forward the final chapter of his book to his literary executor, namely myself.

Wolfgang is dead. It's an undeniable fact, yet unbelievable as I write this, pausing to look out over a sleeping city north of the Arctic Circle at midnight, in the week when the sun reaches the limits of its declination. As yesterday, so no doubt it will be tomorrow, a fiery orange ball, hanging over the shining rooftops and deserted streets of Archangel. Today, as yesterday at this hour, I feel him standing at my back, urging me to publish and damn anyone in his way. It seems clear he'll haunt me every midnight to come, wherever I am, till it's done. Hopefully then his spirit will rest. But Wolfgang was always so quixotic, you could never be sure of anything with him, except timekeeping and dogged persistence.

Why emeralds, you may ask, and why that hotel room in Bogota? Money, of course, or filthy lucre as he would call it, when bailiffs were threatening. Funds with which to buy back his wife's trust. A cash pipeline, as he described it that last night in New York when I warned him not to go. Placing the manuscript in my hands he extracted the promise I would get it published if he failed to return. I – the cockroach of his tale – was his witness, he said, I should have written it, saved him a deal of labour, then he would not have had to hire a deranged secretary. It was my fault, he said, that everything had gone to shit, for the day I left the castle his formerly bounteous luck turned sour. Then he apologized for dumping the manuscript on me, saying I was the one good man he had ever known, and even though a lowly roach, I was still his brother, he insisted, before adding, with uncharacteristic honesty ...

'No, no, Stop typing please Za-Za, PLEASE, I need another.'

'That will cost you more porridge.'

'No problem. Just get chopping them out...'

'Sure thing, massa ...'

'Ah, now that really hit the spot. Man this spike is good. Meant to ask you ah... How much has Skull got in his, um, diplomatic bag?'

gnomepoleon

The mystery of I

DAMNED IF I DO, DAMNED IF I DON'T
by Hubert W. Smith
- Prologue -

Perhaps it were better had I never begun this account. Trouble was always a dog's hot breath on my shoulder. Yea, every time I began the arduous task of writing, a hound of chaos in the form of a lovely woman would come seeking me out, bringing a distaff*[1] in her baggage. When I was not looking, she'd set it up in my yielding earth to serve as a lightning rod, to communicate the anger of the gods, and the manuscript was rent apart, whereupon I was forced to begin again.

For my third attempt, I have set up a work room in a lead-lined crypt in the mausoleum of my wife's ancestors and made arrangements that food and other essentials should be lowered through a grating by a mute hunchback of indeterminate age, answering to the name of Roach. He, according to the Chronicles of the Castle, has been in her family's service for at least three generations.

My first attempt was writ in stone quarried from a storm-lashed headland - Norway one direction, Newfoundland another. Each block bound to its fellow by a special mortar, fine as any optician's cement, of ingredients

---

[1] *Distaff: A pole from which thread is drawn in the spinning of yarns. The gyroscopic distaff, mirroring as it does the rotation of the Earth, is, some say, the superior, in potency of the warlock's rod (see Jessop's account of the Trial of Kate Horner, the Red Witch of Wanlockhead, in 'The Ritual Significance of Cultish Objects'. Published by Harriman of Harrogate, 1902).

I am pledged never to divulge, mixed to proportions set down by the stone masons who built the great cathedrals of the Kingdom to last a thousand years. Sadly, however, despite all my care, that manuscript remains unfinished and lies in ruins in a corner of that northern land known as the Kingdom.

My second attempt was dashed on those same rocks, the splintered wreckage of its ship's timbers long since rotted. A siren looms in the sinking shifting sands of memory, cackling yet weeping, the first of three lovelies turned hags, whose cobweb promises ensnared poor Macbeth, delivering him to his doom.

So where was I? You may have gained a first impression, vouchsafed from my words, that I am a misogynist, a hater of women, and trouble was brought to my doorstep through my own actions and not the agency of the fair sex. On the second score, you may be right, but not with the first. My real mother was a saint, if only because she put up with my father, short time though it was, according to the people who knew her.

My one clear memory of her is being carried in the basket of her bicycle as she pedalled down a narrow country lane between brick walls fragrant with lilac and honeysuckle. The special little blue flowers, we had picked earlier, which she made me promise to always remember, were carefully tucked in the basket, down by my woolly legs. I liked gripping the wickerwork rim of the basket, feeling my cheeks puffing out, and roaring into the wind. Her laughter rang like bells, and then the special blue flowers were spinning in the air. That's where the memory ends, falling into unfathomable blue. My lovely mother was killed by a car speeding in the opposite direction, up the narrow lane. Sometime later I was found, miraculously not a scratch or bruise on me, gurgling happily in a meadow, after being flung over a wall by the force of the impact. I remember nothing of that part, nor the crash, except a vague memory of flying in a shower of blue forget-me nots.

My father soon remarried. My replacement mother came with three ugly daughters. The eldest, two and a half years older than me, was a big thug, but a coward too, fortunately. The younger two, both thin as whips, were pathetic tell-tales with no imagination. SHE talked about love and good intentions a lot and was forever fussing with my half-sisters. Brushing their long hair every morning after breakfast, the thug's blonde hair platted into pigtails. They got driven to and from school every day, but I had to take the bus there and walked the three miles home because I'd spend the fare during the day.

They had music lessons after school, on Tuesdays and Thursdays, at a music academy where I was supposed to meet them. The building was next to a cinema. Around the entrance were posters of forthcoming films which featured green castles against lurid red skies, and bearded men lunging at women with bloody knives, which my stepmother always rushed past because she hated beards on men. I was supposed to sit in the foyer of the stupid music academy for one whole hour, waiting for my sisters, having to put up with the screeches of violins and muffled plonking of pianos from behind doors of the long corridor that stretched away from the foyer into the dimness of low wattage lighting that had been regulation since the Civil War.

From behind one door, however, issued different sounds; just discernible galloping hooves, footsteps on stairs, the cry of a wolf, an animal panting, drips echoing in a tunnel...

The dripping tunnel, I discovered, was actually a dark passage between the buildings, and the animal breathing was me, navigating pots and pans in the darkness, set out to catch the drips from sodden boards in the ceiling. Finally, reaching the end of the tunnel, I came upon a door, which was ajar. I had found the secret way into the forbidden cinema. On the wall on the other side of the door, an emergency exit neon sign cast a purple glow into the gloom beyond, outlining hunched figures scattered among the rows, who were in for the second afternoon screening of the featured certificate X horror film. When I took my seat that Tuesday, the opening credits were already rolling.

The story was very confusing, but interesting. Appropriately, because the film was much concerned with hairy legs, it started with a warning about a good man cursed at birth by a gipsy woman. He grows up big and tall. At night, he says his prayers, but nevertheless when the moon is full and the wolfbane blooms, hair grows thick on his legs, like mine. Strange things happen. He talks with his father for one, and for two, falls in love. Murders he didn't commit are blamed on him. So many that he starts to believe his accusers. But that comes later. First the good man has to return to a castle, catch-up with his father, who is a laird, get bitten by a werewolf, the son of the gipsy woman who was the cause of all the fun. However, I missed the next part, because an usherette with a torch shone her light and, in a loud whisper, told me to leave. It was before the blood scene, which I caught up on the Thursday showing, the next time my sisters had lessons at the music school.

Sundays after church, Mother invited friends from the congregation to performances of Mozart minuets. The sisters frantically bowing and plucking on violins and cello, and Mother pling-plonking away on the Steinway that had had to be delivered through the drawing room's bay window on the first floor because it was too grand to pass up our stairs. I didn't go. Nor to church, not after *that* Sunday dinner, when the minister, who had lingered after the musical performance, was asked by Mother to say grace, much to my Father's ire.

Into the silence which followed, before my father had a chance to put a forkful into his moustachioed mouth, I loudly declared I was a rapist (of course meaning atheist), demanding on moral grounds to be recused from communion, which I said was against my animal beliefs as a wolf. The minister, who I had been addressing, crossed himself. My step-mother hid her face for shame. The sisters shrieked for glee. My father called for order, banging his fist on the table, only adding to the general hub-bub. But as per usual I persisted and finally got my way, after threatening to expose my legs to the congregation, which was probably just as well because if not I had decided to steal onto a ship to Canada, where I had an idea the Hudson Bay Company might employ me as a beaver trapper, even though I was then only 11 years old.

I was in the dog-house for months, but thankfully free of God in church on Sundays. I was well in with the bad boys, who lived in the crowded tenements of nearby streets, where they shared beds with younger brothers, even sisters, in one-roomed flats called single ends. They soon called me mad, because I never turned a dare down. My first was to steal the bell from the counter of the local police station, which I did when reporting seeing a missing cat under a seat of the No. 5 bus. The cat in question was pictured on the lamppost outside the station. More thefts followed, torture implements and appointment cards from a dentist later arrested for unnecessarily filling children's teeth - including mine - with mercury amalgam, which can cause delusions and even madness in later years ...

... the torture implements came in handy with the two younger sisters, and the appointment cards got me out of school lessons I didn't like, which were most of them. A receiver ripped from a telephone box near the family home, on which I made mystery calls from behind my desk, entertained my classmates during boring lessons, as I took instructions from alien spymasters.

Extracts from the Journals of the MAD Dentist

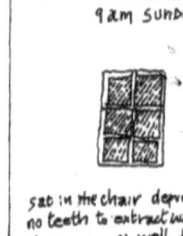

9 am SUNDAY

sat in the chair depressed no teeth to extract watched the rain... ah well fresh teeth in the morning

9 am MONDAY

the patient sits in the chair fingers touching air footsteps approach

FEEL anything sir

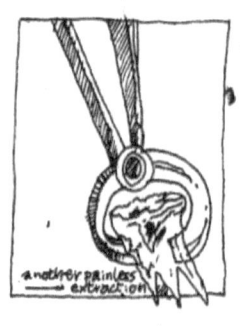

another painless extraction

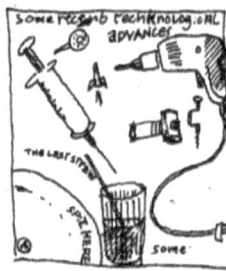

Some recent technological advances

THE LAST STRAW

GOES HERE

some

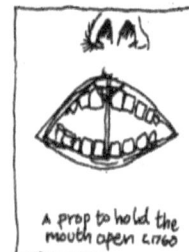

A prop to hold the mouth open c.1760

5.05 pm count days takings 23 .... not bad

Let me in I'll only pick your nose

To supplement my meagre 6d pocket money, which had remained the same since my 6th birthday, I stole books from a store that had a second-hand department, who bought back the same books for a third of cost, which I thought an excellent arrangement, till I took a call from Alien High Command and was advised to find something else worthwhile to do. I had an assegai spear from a missionary relative, which I would take to the nearby park and throw into trees, when bored. The claymore sword came later, from a regimental pipe major who gave me bagpipe lessons in the funny little house by the No.5 bus stop. On his good days, when he wasn't drunk, he told me stories of life in the Army, pausing to have me light the cigarettes he chain-smoked, his stories getting darker and the smoke thicker as the lesson progressed. But at least in those lessons I didn't get beaten over the knuckles with his special chanter of African iron wood, kept for the purpose. It had belonged to his teacher, for getting the fingering of a reel or jig wrong, which I invariably did, in fear of his alcoholic rages.

Then when I was supposed to be at home practicing the Kingdom's version of pan pipes, and promised hellfire next lesson if I didn't, I was outside getting yelled at by neighbours, who took exception to my wolf's legs and the claymore which I waved at them when I skipped along the stone walls between their gardens, a sure-fire escape route from home. Hid from them all. They were nuts. But at least I have my memory of that bicycle ride to warm me in these crypts where lately I find myself, the sweet scents of spring in the wind, and my mother's lovely laughter as she pedalled. I feel lucky to have that memory, for I was only eighteen months when the accident happened. Her blind optimism I have brought to every new relationship.

Where then lies the problem, and from whence does it come? A part, grown wary this last decade, holds that the women I have loved were but damaged vehicles like myself, and the pain came through mixed sorrows, curdling our milk and spoiling our daily bread.

Of my father I will say this: here was a man whose sentences might last a page or two, and each paragraph a ream or more. If I shouted into the driving blast of his monologue, he would cast back, with ne'er a let-up of the gale, 'you'll get your say bye and bye...'

Head of the Table.

Or if interrupted a second time, his already ruddy face would be eclipsed ... nay, engulfed in an ascending thundercloud of blood. He might shriek an imprecation to the highest heaven, raise the cutlery from the family table, which though thick oak from the mast of a slaver ship captained by a distant ancestor, always jumped to the beat of his fist, but ne'er once would he stop the floodtide.

When, mid-monologue, a glass of water was raised to ruddy lips to sooth his overused throat, or, the meal being finished, he paused to light his pipe, a chance came to venture an opinion of my own, scarce three words would I have said before my father would pounce.

'There was this man-'

'WHICH MAN!' my father would roar, and the cutlery would dance.

Stubbornly, I would continue, 'I read somewhere there was this man said ...'

'Damn-it boy!' he yelled, waving away clouds of pipe smoke to better see me across the table, 'How many times must I tell you not to say *this* man and to sit up straight when you are answering questions. Now what was the title of the book, when was it published, and what exactly did you read?'

For my father everything had to be cross-referenced, and this was why his sentences were so convoluted and interminable. Endlessly pedantic, facts for him were an army of foot-soldiers marching out his mouth, cock-roach fashion, each following the one before, and of course arranged according to rank.

There was *this* man I met once, not known by my father, but in one important respect similar, as you will see bye and bye. Placid Ted was an upholsterer to trade, a home-loving man who by his own admission had never looked at a woman, apart from his wife, with a lustful eye.

I listened with half a mind as he meandered the war years when doo-dlebugs rained on London's East End, and so I missed the vital connection. It seemed that somewhere placid Ted's disposition had changed. A word misconstrued, a van parked in the street outside his workshop - anything could turn him homicidal. It was only because these rages departed sud-denly as they descended and were so incandescent that men much bigger

(Placid Ted was a small man) would turn and run. Or a sudden noise might waken his senses so that Placid Ted would wonder what he was doing half-dressed, out in the street, a hammer in his hand.

Placid Ted told me that when a hospital surgeon cut out his thyroid, 'It wuz the soize of a calf's liver.' The scar on his neck looked like he'd narrowly survived a garrotting.

When he was convalescing from the operation, his wife casually mentioned, 'Wot wiv all the to-do of you in 'ospital,' she'd forgotten to mention that a son had smashed his favourite ornament while playing football in the lounge.

Instead of flying into a rage as he would have before the operation, Placid Ted replied, 'Ow down't yew worry luv, we'll foind anuvver wun, just the soime, yew'll see.'

At that his wife burst into tears. 'That's me Ted,' she sobbed, dabbing a hankie to her eyes, 'Oi've gotten me Ted back, efter awl these years.'

In his late fifties, my father too had a section of his thyroid surgically removed. After the operation, my step-sisters said his disposition was much changed for the better. However, that didn't apply where I was concerned. It seems that at least as far as sons and fathers are concerned, the habits of a lifetime can take a lifetime to die.

Last week, while travelling on the Underground, without warning I was possessed by an intense loathing of *this* man seated next to me. Something about his florid face, the pin stripes of his immaculate pressed city suit, his stiff white shirt, the old boy school tie, possibly the hairs on the back of his hands, which were thick and black. As I tried to discern what lay behind my outbreak of irrational hostility against this man who, after all, was a complete stranger, I noticed a tiny flea emerge from under a shirt cuff, and its tiny legs tense...

Before it could spring the gap between us, I jumped up, and to the puzzlement of the passengers packing the carriage, shrieked at the man, 'You fucking shit, get away from me!' I continued this way until the train had stopped, the carriage emptied and I found myself alone, though I did perceive the platform outside packed with staring faces. Commuters thick as South American flies on the only turd in town.

Tomorrow I am going to send word up to the hunchback, whose real name I have suddenly realized I have never known, telling him to deliver a note to my doctor. I'm worried about my thyroid, which has started to throb. Perhaps he can diagnose my condition through the grating. On reflection, I think I will postpone the visit. Verbosity, they say, when held on a tight rein, is the writer's good friend. And writing, they say, is the last resort of a scoundrel. We'll say no more about that for now at least, I have enough of my wife's relatives around in this mausoleum to remind me of my failings.

THE PORRIDGE CAULDRON

by Dwane Earl McHay

The Bard of Bad –

'And who is going to make the Porridge for our tea?
Everyone, including you and me...'

Popular song, early 21st century, from the Album by the
Screaming Zits, Armageddon out-a here.'

'From the Yird we shall hang, the ee's plucked ooot wir shriven
corpses, by black craws o' the field, 'til oor flesh is judged ripe for the pot.'

Anonymous Kingdom Ballad, late 15th Century.

It has just gone two am in the morning, and in the turret bedroom Brünhilda is gripping patchwork bedcovers for dear life, unable to shut out
the sounds of the night - above, swifts nesting in the eves; outside, in the
woods below the railway embankment, the foxes rutting again; down in the
courtyard, Mickey shuffling about in the airstream caravan - he was ever a
poor sleeper. Told her so himself, in the kitchen when she made him cocoa
to warm him up, after she found him dead drunk on the road up to the
castle. He made her laugh, joking about the lady of the castle and the joiner.
She finds him a bit rough though, a jackal to her wolf. What is it about
him, she wonders? Perhaps the way he moves, when dancing at parties in
the great hall, like he has rubber bones, or after a fall bounces right back
up, as happens quite a lot when he is drunk. He always dresses down, in
sombre browns or black... well, not his blue jeans, which are wranglers according to the Monday washing woman, who collects the castle laundry.
Last Tuesday, handing back the clothes, she whispered, as she does when
passing on a titbit from the wives of Snaresburgh, 'word is, ma'am, he's got a
huge dongle,'

Brünhilda wanted to ask what that meant, but feeling unable to do so,
only nodded, as ever instantly regretting her silence. Never mind, she thinks.
Least said sooner mended, as Nanny would say. She resolves to look it up in the
dictionary, try not to get daunted by so many words. The woman is a terrible gossip. So it is good she doesn't know that Mickey is a real outlaw, because loose lips sink ships in the Atlantic, all the time. Actually on the run
from the authorities, having jumped bail, which she understood was rather
high, and to do with cricket stumps, in court procedure. But we only
learned that after he arrived at the castle bedraggled, looking for work. She
remembers it was lashing a gale, and there was a power cut when he
knocked. Though the hour was late, his timing was perfect, because workers

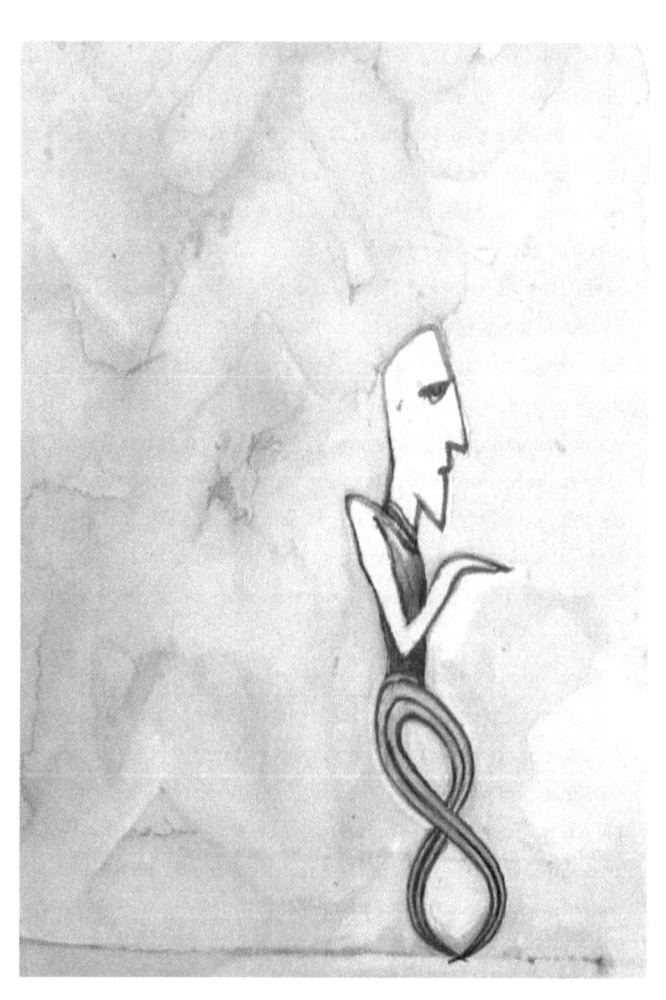

are hard to find in the countryside as poor Papa would say whenever one left. She'd cautioned Wolfgang the same, and he'd returned to bed grumpy, saying he was not in the mood, after settling Mickey into the caravan which the sisters conveniently had vacated only that morning, and all because he had stubbed his paw in the darkness, negotiating the elephant hat stand in the hall when answering the door.

Brünhilda recalls Wolfgang wanted to get rid of Mickey after finding him drunk and then hearing from a third party - how I hate that term - about the warrant out for his arrest, but she insisted he stayed. Surprised herself, going against him like that. Reminded him that the Bandit King in 1744 was just one of the fugitives from justice granted sanctuary in the castle over the centuries, and saying to do otherwise would be to affront the laws of Haggard hospitality, and she wouldn't allow it. Really put her heel down that time. Wolfgang was speechless, for once, which was reward in itself and felt like a first step towards reclaiming herself, as the Sisters of the Soil so often advised her to do.

Besides, Brünhilda reasons, Mickey works hard and deserves every penny he is paid, for all he has been sneaking bottles of her hedge wine from the pantry when he runs out of money to spend in the pub. He never moans his lot, clearly cares about Wolfgang even if he sometimes sneers, and is generally fun to be with. Certainly, no one else around to hear to her troubles since Nanny died, in the same week the sisters left. So sad, unlike when her Mama died, and finally got her wish, being buried in the Südatenland in a Mennonite churchyard near where she had been born, at last with the congregation that'd banished her for marrying poor Papa.

More banshee laughter from the woods. Nanny always said that foxes were witches in animal skins, and when they shrieked like that they were doing wicked things.

Closer, at her side, her wolf, paddled his paws in his sleep, moaning and making odd barks. Having that serial dream again, she supposed, acidly. It was the one he always bored on about over his porridge the next morning, like he first did their first proper holiday, except then being Greece it was poached eggs, olives, feta, and roasted pine nuts stuffed with vine leaves or perhaps the other way round. They'd eaten in the hotel breakfast room with the big window, overlooking that gorge in Crete. By now she had his dream down pat she'd heard it so often. How the hound of hell, gnashing three sets of great teeth, had come in the dead of the night, demanding restitution for something he was supposed to have done, he didn't know what. Raced right out of the gorge at him, he said, which was a crack in the world descending to the pits of Hades.

She sighed, knowing that in a few hours, at breakfast, he'd add another detail to the sorry saga, and pin it with a little paper flag on the maps he had pieced together across the length of the kitchen wall, twelve and a half inches to the mile,

The maps are crossed by strings so taught that you only have to look at them and they twang. Supposedly they trace ley lines that connect sites like burial grounds, cross roads, mountain summits, watchtowers, even a telephone exchange and a slaughter house, all mentioned in his expanding serial dream. Also pinned to the maps are press cuttings, letters to the editor, death notices, photos and scraps of paper, on which he has scribbled notes. There is even a head of wheat and a tiny packet of dry berries from a Neolithic mound in a little transparent packet. One string he has chalked blue. Sometimes it glows at night, he says, but she thinks that is when he has been working on his maps too long. This string connects the castle to the family mausoleum on Mourning Rock Hill and other places of significance, in the south east of the Kingdom, where it ends, with a flag on a sea cliff, marking the furthest point of land in the Kingdom, from where presumably it passes on to other parts.

Apparently the ley line is the ancient Viam Mortuorum mentioned in the castle's chronicles, which he tells her is Latin for *The Way of the Dead*, and which points to Jerusalem from the site of the first Castle Haggard, before the quarry blew its crag away. A problem, he says, because the famous crystalline pink granite of the crags has been reduced to gravel. It is that gravel which we spread on the forking paths in the garden so the maze that the Sisters of the Soil laid (with such care measuring every angle and turn of the paths with theodolites, and goodness knows whatnot) could trap ghosts. Convincing her, if she needed it, she married a complete *head-case*, which she doesn't having firmly made up her mind on the subject in the first week of her marriage.

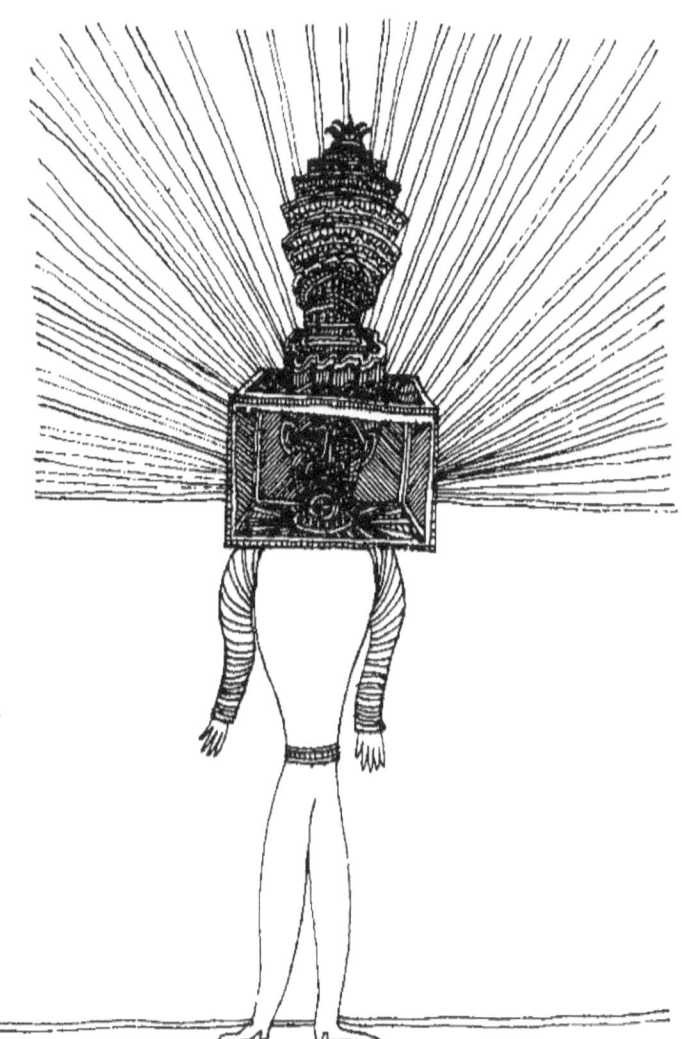

Now he thinks the dream is to do with a 15th century burial, disturbed when he blew up the pig sties in the great hall, starting his renovations with a bang. He believes it might be the missing crypt where the unsanctified sinners of the family were buried during the time of the witch trials.

But, with luck, this time the three-headed hound will chase him over the gorge. She imagines them plunging, still grappling, gyring down towards a spitting pit of fire, and the devil, a trident in hand, impatiently tapping a cloven hoof, waiting beside an altar of skulls to pronounce the sentence of doom.

Knowing Wolfgang, however, he'd somehow escape his fetters, clamber out of the pit, piss into the fire, kick over the altar of skulls, steal the trident, and, waving it like a trophy of war, burst back into her life to make it hell again, no matter how much she gives him, always wanting more for his unfinished renovations which have almost bankrupted them.

She should have listened to Papa's warnings. Normally a man of few words, he really blew his top that time. How did he phrase it? *'Low breeding and nothing between the ears but an ill wind, the puff of his foolish pretensions issuing his lupine backside, an ingrate like all of his kind. Had we lived in a better century, my gal, I'd have shot the carpet bagger when he first stepped onto the drawbridge, and you'd have come to thank me.'* Yes that was about it, she thinks, but she's not sure about the last part, considering by that time her Papa had moved to the bungalow, and the castle hadn't had a drawbridge since the moat was filled during the False Peace of the 15th century, when everything got slack and the Red Duchess held a great banquet which beggared her descendants in ways that were never explained.

Her portrait had always been turned to the wall in the great hall, a talking point when visitors came to call at the castle and the silences got long.

Very long in her parents' generation. But not since the renovations, Wolfgang, in a rare show of forethought, having removed it from the great hall with the other portraits to one of his stores before the nice quarry man blew up the horrible pig sties. She must dig it out, she reminds herself, for the 'nth time, if only to see if the Red Duchess really looked like her, as dear old aunt Nessie once said. But forget that for the moment, she thinks. In this one thing at least, poor old Papa was right, she should never have married him. Any moment now he'd start paddling her into a smaller portion of the bed than the current third which was his idea of sharing, damn him.

Hearing renewed bouts of banshee cackling announcing more penetration in the dark wood – to judge by new crescendos, the vixen being pack raped? Brünhilda imagines the pack climbing on each other in their frustration to get at the bitch in their centre. She reflects despite his patronymic, her husband is really a dog, in that no different from every other man, all of them dogs. Possessing as they do the scratching rituals, beastly ways and pack mentality, comparing the size of their dicks, the same, being similarly obsessed with faecal matter. Why else would they fart so, or when drunk place their vulgar signatures on every phallic landmark, dominate their bitches, and vie with each other for the same.

Staring up at the skylight and a waning sickle moon emerging from behind scudding clouds, she wonders what animal best represents her female spirit. After hesitating over a moth attracted to a sputtering flame, her sex life these past months, she settles on a butterfly. Herself, that moment, reflected in the dark glass of the skylight, a small presence above covers that flap like night wings. On her face, her mouth a purse string, the lines of her thirties drawing in, every day more her like miserable mother who suffered from homesickness for her Mennonite relatives who cast her out, and sometimes stayed in this same bed for months refusing to get up except to use the bedpan. Could she end up like that, she wonders, be forever trapped in this castle she no longer recognised since Wolfgang started his endless *renovations*? All because she once stupidly remarked that it was a white elephant, and no one in their right mind would ever pay money to visit a castle with a quarry eating the crags behind it. She can't remember whose idea it was to turn the pig sties into artists' cottages, and the clock tower into weaving studios, but he insists it was hers, when she complains about the dirt he trails from his never-ending *renovations* into the kitchen of the big house.

It was ages since she'd visited her father's grave, as she regularly used to do, the ancient key heavy in her hand, descending the worn steps to the metal door with the rusty grill. Behind it her ancestors' sarcophaguses were racked like musty old bottles in the groined vaults. The pillars processed into darkness and further crypts, where it had become dangerous to go, because of the seeping ground gas from many years of the quarry blasting Haggard Hill, fissuring the bedrock. The eldest sons' had armorial shields, names and pedigrees carved on the walls above their recesses. Only the names of the rest were incised above theirs: sons and mothers, sisters and cousins, scoundrels and spendthrifts, generation upon generation of the family, combed in perfect repose in their recesses around the vaults.

Perhaps what she was feeling was the guilt of a disobedient daughter who went against her father's will – never more so than by marrying. *Was his fatal attack of apoplexy brought on by the prospect of leading me down the aisle at church?* He was such a stickler for tradition and would never have refused her that. Was his rage then the real reason? if so, she'd committed, what did they call it, regicide? – such a horrible word. She hoped not, dear Papa, she'd hate to think that her marriage was the cause.

When she was little, and her mother was in her miserable Mennonite wimple and drab smock, weeding in the vegetable garden or chasing out the black-faced sheep she said were sent by Satan back out through the gap in the wall where the South Gate had been breached during the Great Siege of '33, sometimes he would call her his wee mouse and kindly pat her head with his broad hand. That was in the great hall, as he stood before a blazing log fire in the big hearth, by the armorial mantle with the shield and crossed swords of Haggard, surrounded by portraits of their ancestors, with one turned to the wall. He'd sip his first whisky of the afternoon, smoking through the amber mouthpiece of the old meerschaum pipe he'd got from the man in his regiment who'd put the 'cuffs on a high-ranking Nazi who Papa had known in Germany before the War, when Nazis weren't all bad. The pipe made the smoke spiral when he puffed, and the black briar grip was carved into the body of a wee Turkish man, perfect in every detail. The bowl was his turban, which the wee man held between his delicate hands.

Queer though the Meerschaum was, with the hard eyes of the wee man staring back at you and his crooked smile, the spiralling action of the smoke through the coiled turban, and briar's doubtful provenance in the Black Forest where it was said the Devil had a castle, it was still Papa's favourite pipe, so she placed it in his hand on his breast, in the open coffin in the crypt, before stealing a forbidden kiss from his pellucid lips. She was glad she had, even though the lips were stone cold and made her shiver whenever she thought of them. Then, a tearful last goodbye, hearing her tremulous sobs echoing the vaults some time after. Finally closing the hinged top panel of the coffin with the sound of doom. Though she tried to shut it softly, still it echoed.

All that long night, faithful to the Haggard family tradition which ordained that firstborns, be they sons or daughters, maintain the *vigil*, lest the tutelary spirits take their predecessor's shade before the cock crows, on the third day of the *lying-in*. After which, tout-suite, a short service, then the old Laird, sealed in the inner coffin, was hurriedly entombed in his stone sarcophagus, long prepared by the masons of Snaresburgh Lodge No. 9. The new Laird was then installed in the castle, entering by the South Gate, the same way the coffin had left, before the sun passed behind Mourning Rock Hill and the day was out. In her case, this new laird was her husband. And all because firstborn daughters couldn't be lairds, as was ordained, by whom or when, no one ever could say. Still the traditions must be adhered to, she reflected, grimly, with a mental nod to her new friends in the Sisters of Soil Collective, incomprehensible though the Haggard family customs and obligations were.

Looking back, she'd only got through the dreadful night by taking pills from one of the bottles in her mother's medicine cabinet. The label read, 'for narcolepsy'. She didn't know what that was exactly, except it was to do with sleeping, which mother did a lot, so took a handful. It was good that she had, because most of the night was a blur, as was the burial the next day, thankfully.

Affection came difficult to him, she realized now, but now she was grateful for what little she'd had. If only she had taken his advice. She could feel him rolling in his grave even from this distance. His disapproval, spiralling upwards like his pipe smoke used to do under the old roof beams of the great hall, only the black clouds were gathering over the mausoleum, where she would rest in the recess next to his one day.

On the sunless side of Mourning Rock Hill, the pillared vaults now overlooked the great gash of the quarry, and the blood pits, so called because the granite dust blowing in from the long conveyor belts, where the gravel was sifted, and stone wash from the mills in which boulders were crushed and graded, had turned the deep waters flooding the pits carmine red. Too bad, for the growing wound in Haggard Hill interfered with the view of the castle, sheltering in the lee of the railway line embankment in the valley opposite, so green with its ancient woods and bucolic pastures.

Down by the river the blackface sheep and shaggy longhorn cattle grazed contentedly on neaps and cabbage stumps in the flat fields that had been reclaimed from the river. Even the hut and short pier of Snaresburgh's so-called yacht club was visible, though concealed from lower vantage points by the beds of bulrushes, which grew thick along the banks all the way to the small port. There, cranes loaded ships with giant rolls of Cleanoleum to be laid in hospital corridors, schools, offices and penitentiaries around the world, in countries with names that were difficult to remember. The tidal river snaked past the two giant chimney stacks of the Cleanoleum Works, to its source in the Ben Benachie, a high mountain with a glittering peak which, as much as these things can be determined, marked the dead centre of the Kingdom.

It was said that from there, on a clear day, you could read the time on the clock on the Castle Tower. But when poor Papa climbed the mountain, aged only 25, then a junior officer in the army before the Great War, he was temporarily blinded by the mid-day sun reflecting off mica on the summit and had to be carried down by men of his platoon. Which was too bad, because he was supposed to test a theory the peak could be used for communication in the event of enemy invasion, by alternately draping and removing blankets laid on the mica, thereby heliographing signals to a soldier left on lookout sixty miles away in the castle. Papa used to joke that the soldier's ghost was still waiting in the top of the Clock Tower and would continue doing so long after he was gone. But you could see it all from the Mausoleum.

The vegetable garden and maze at the back of the big house was a postage stamp on a picture post card of a much-reduced Eden. Nine tenths of our land had been sold off since the 11th Laird and the castle's heyday, before the Great Banking Crisis of the 17th century when the economy of the country was paralyzed for 50 years and the Laird ran out of gold guineas that had filled the Haggard Kist, more's the pity. Well, Papa was right, it was well past time she made a move, any longer might be too late; but has she the strength?

It is then Brünhilda hears a footfall on the stairs, which is strange because there is no accompanying creak from the steps below. She works herself up on her elbows against the pillows in time to see the carpeted hatch rising, which lifted from below at the touch of a finger, and the counterweight dropping on its rope towards the carpet as, from the dark stairwell stepped a tall slender woman, her features shrouded in cobwebbed lace.

The ghost, if ghost it is, glides in towards the foot of the bed, where it stands, watching. Brünhilda, who has fallen back against the pillows, notes with astonishment it isn't fear she's feeling, but the leaking away of all the loneliness of her years, and at the same time an inflow of strength for what now knows she must do.

Who is she? Brünhilda wonders, as the spectre raises a hand then fades from view. The only sign she was ever there the dead man's brass counterweight slowly swinging back and forth on its rope over the carpet.

Though faded from view, the spectre, who is none other than the shade of the Red Duchess, maintains her vigil, watching until long after Morpheus has reclaimed Brünhilda, who sleeps deeply now, a smile on her lips.

Not so Wolfgang, who remains trapped in a phantom world of his own making. His top lip twitching, beads of sweat stringing his abacus brow, as across his two thirds of the bed falls a long shadow cast by a scimitar moon.

A BLACK DOG TALE
by Kathleen K. McKnightley

Wolfgang is dreaming of dogs – one dog in particular – a singularly large black dog sent to collect his wayward soul.

In his dream, Wolfgang stands in a churchyard before an open grave, clutching ... clutching ... well, clutching nothing, but his hands working as if they did – perhaps the comforting blanket he had as a child? As over the churchyard wall leaps Cerberus, the reclaimer of souls, and Wolfgang into the pit of his own making is falling, falling. With an effort that could have restored the leaning Tower of Pisa to a vertical position, Wolfgang wakes, finds himself bolt upright in bed, his heart racing fit to burst, as from the woods issues another torrid bout of laughter. Then, as the horrid cackling dies, he hears a stray sound outside, below, in the courtyard. Realizing this is no wayward tin can set rolling by the wind, nor a latched gate bumping back against its post, he jumps to his feet on the bed and pushes the skylight above open.

Even before he can put a name on the thing stood very still in the courtyard below, he knows what it is. For there staring back at him, not with eyes so much as with a black malevolent radiance, is the uncertain outline of the same dog he'd dreamed. But he knows this is no dream.

'GET THE FUCK OFF!' Wolfgang's cry is atavistic, a sound wrung out from deep within. Then he feels Brünhilda at his side, her slim form annealed to his flesh, warm against his skin, adding her voice to his, as down in the courtyard the black dog turns and more ripples than runs past the cottages, its outline uncertain, drawing flitting shadows from the fields beyond. Then the instant the banshee cackling of foxes peaks – whoof! the monstrous Black Dog is gone as if it never was.

moby dick + moby cunt

Wolfgang and Brünhilda fuck then – a cold sweaty hands groping distant kind of fuck. As he reaches climax and moves to kiss her, she turns her head away.

Lips brushing her ear, he breathes the old spell of binding, 'I love you,' and more of the same as she fails to reply. Then he is spent, words and seed falling on stony ground.

'Wolfgang...' she says, and his heart leaps at the faraway sound of her voice under the covers.

'Yes, my darling?'
'Pass the Kleenex will you, and turn out the light.'

Later, standing before the old gilt mirror in the turret bathroom, examining his chin, Wolfgang notes a spot which wasn't there the day before. Not a pluke exactly, for though red and throbbing, it is hard and scaly to the touch, and feels more like grit which has rooted to his chin.

Wolfgang runs his mind over events in the bedroom. He'd felt such inexplicable rage he'd had to jump from the bed and immediately leave the room. For why; she'd only asked for a tissue. But it was more than that, for there it was written across the grey blue irises of her watery eyes that he'd never measure up as a laird, and she saw him as an indentured servant kept around to service her needs when not refurbishing the buildings.

In the turret bathroom, looking into the speckled depths of the old mirror, Wolfgang rubs his 3 am stubble with his palm. His cheek has gone numb. Stress, that's all it is, he tells himself – the same as brought on by novocaine after a visit to the mad dentist, filling his teeth with more mercury amalgam, only it's the pressure of taking his five-year renovations through to completion, that has caused the numbness. He'll have to be careful. Just then in bed he'd wanted to sink his wolf teeth into her wineglass neck and bite her jugular.

Was that me? he asked his reflection, the mirror. 'No, not me,' he said aloud, '*no exist nada,*' as if by addressing his beastly other self in a foreign language he could exorcise his dog demon.

Inside a neat picket fence, at the end of a short path of crazy paving, Wolfgang was wondering just what he was doing out in his dressing gown and slippers, holding a bottle, standing before the airstream, resembling more a silver grub from space in the darkness than a caravan capable of bunking six at a pinch. Gods bane, no, what was he thinking of? Before he could turn on a paw and pad back down the forget-me-not-speckled path laid by the sisters, a door like a submarine hatch cracked open, red light bisected three white steps, and Mickey's tousled head and pale face stuck out.

'I heard ye,' he said. 'Why didnae youz just come in?' He scowled. 'Youz alwus did 'afore.'

'Ay well, this time it's different, Mickey. I wanted to talk. Here. I've brought this.' Wolfgang held up the whisky bottle. 'What say we share it?'

Crouched by the open stove, raking the coals with a poker, Mickey said, 'Weill, talk then, but first gie me a hit o' that bottle. Here, fill me up.' He held out his *billy can*, used for brewing tea, according to the venerable traditions of builders huts.

'So...' Clinking can to bottle, Mickey sat down on the rumpled bed next to Wolfgang. 'Whit's this a' aboot?' he said, his gaunt face red in the light of the bedside lamp as he leaned in.

Wolfgang expelled a withheld breath through gritted teeth. 'Me and Brünhilda haven't been getting on too well.'

'I could haee telt ye that fuckin' years ago, when I first worked here.'

'It's a recent thing. We were fine before.'

'No accordin' tae her. She's was cryin' oan my shoulder that first week.'

'Aye, but if you remember, that coincided with the start of the renovations. It's been tough on both of us.'

'Tougher on her.'

'Come off it, Mickey. What does she have to do, raking the forking paths in the garden with the weekend lesbians, a bit of housework, maybe jam-making or home-brewing as the fancy takes her, some cooking, Cockroach scurrying at her beck and call. Whereas my pots and pans are beams twenty feet long, bricks and slabs for plates, and I have to manage squads of men still half-pissed from the night before because no one else from Snaresburgh bar the alkies are prepared to put in a day's work. My equivalent of clearing up the kitchen at the end of the day is tamping tons of spoil back into holes after digging up the drains, because the Sisters of the Soil's spinach tampons have been blocking them again. It's worse on me...'

Taking the bottle from Wolfgang's grasp, Mickey shook his head. He refilled his billy can, an uncharacteristic smile playing rubber lips.

'Alright then,' Wolfgang conceded, 'it's me ... I'm the one to blame. Is that how you see it?'

Mickey shrugged.

Wolfgang took another swig from the bottle. 'You know how it is in the building trade, Mickey, if you don't act hard, everyone takes you for a mug. I've been having to act that way since starting the renovations, and now I can't get the mask off. Like I've become that mean bastard. It's affecting my relationship with Brünhilda.' He raised the bottle again.

'Here, pass me that. I'm no goin' tae sit here an' watch ye drink it a' by yersel' ...'

'Reversed roles, huh?'

'Eh, an' whit dae ye mean by that?'

'Well normally it's me watching you drown your sorrows ...'

'An' jest what dae ye ken aboot my sorrows? Oan the run after busting a policeman's jaw, who only deserved it. Naewhere safe, Belfast, Glasgow,

London, Hamburg, aye an' Snaresburgh doon the road. Everywhaur the same. Ower high hedges, an' behind picture windaes, posh folk like youz an' Brünhilda unwrappin' presents yer hale lives, one long Christmas and ye dinnae even realize it!'

'Aye, an' I can just see you,' Wolfgang chuckled, 'Mickey the universal hobo, lost in suburbia, by the light of the silvery moon, plenty of nothing in your hand.' His voice hardened. 'Well for your information, Mickey, over this castle's walls and behind that turret window the fire's going cold, and I don't know what I can do.' He sighed self-pityingly. 'Brünhilda doesn't even talk to me these days.'

'That's 'cause wi' youz it's no a hoose like everywan else. It's got tae be a big castle wi' an ivory tower planted in the middle. Ye should try comin' doon oaf it once in a fuckin' while.'

'Is that how you see the place? I thought you might understand. All these years I've been fired up by the idea of sharing the place when I get to the end of these renovations.' He shrugged. 'How else could I use all this?' he said, waving a hand about.

'Oh yea?'

'Like filling all the studios and workshops with real artists who've had to push against the grain, working in poky city studios like rats in holes. Let them show what they are really capable of with decent facilities, living in the countryside, breathing fresh air instead of polluted fumes. I even thought, once Brünhilda and I have set all this up, we might fuck off round the world for a bit and leave them all to get on with it.' He shrugged, benevolently. 'Come back after a couple of years ...'

a number four Iron Sam ✦

'Aye I can just see youz wi' a golden state tan, shoulderin' yer golf clubs through the castle door in'a Malibu shirt, welcomed by yer arty friends, supping yer special porridge with silver spoons ye were a' born wi'.' Mickey took another hit on the bottle. 'But a'fore that, cunt,' he spat to the side, 'youz should try comin' doon oaff o' that ivory tower and see the wurrld like the rest o' uz.'

'For example?' Wolfgang said, trying to ignore Mickey's spittle sizzling persistently on the hot stove.

'Like getting' fuckin pissed with the lads doon at the Tally-Ho Friday nights.'

'Aye.' Wolfgang jerked his thumb in the direction of the big house and his sleeping wife. 'And she'd be sure to appreciate that, me reeling back to the castle after, drunk as a lord, like you do every time you get paid.'

Mickey's rubber face twisted. 'Is that the fuckin' end o' that whisky?' He tilted the empty bottle in his hand, peering into its glassy depths. 'Bastards...'

'I've another stashed in the big house where you wouldn't find it.' Wolfgang stood up, noting, of the general disorder, the heaped blankets, the sour smell of damp socks and underpants in corners, so different from the fragrant lesbians, who kept the airstream spotless when they stayed. Every day flowers in the windows, the cut-glass always sparkling, its aluminium panels so polished it was hard to look at the caravan in bright sunlight.

'Come on.' Wolfgang shook his head, restraining the urge to snap his fingers. 'It's warmer in the kitchen.' He nodded towards the stove. 'That fire of yours is fucking useless.'

SPEED IS CALLED FOR
by Hector D. McBraine

It is morning, creeping on nine by the old railway clock in the darkened kitchen. A sunbeam edges the window blind, illuminating the near corner of the assemblage of maps where the long blue string passes over a place called Kingsknowe. Over by the big old solid fuel cooker, Mickey is flat on his back, his head tipping the wooden bench, one finger hooked in the neck of an empty bottle, his open mouth exposing a full set of nicotine-stained teeth.

Sounds: just the slow ticking of the clock, soft purring from an old cat on the topmost shelf of the old pine dresser, and Mickey's erratic breathing. Outside, the fleeting conversations of birds, the drone of a car passing beyond the siege wall. More distantly, a low ratchet rumble, as always five days out of seven, from behind the railway embankment – as ever the quarry leviathan's teeth, grinding the granite of the crags.

Then, three floors up, in the turret bedroom, there was movement, as Wolfgang woke a third time and realized, unless he got going and pronto, he was going to miss the moment and the train of providence before it left the station that morning. He believed that no matter who stood in his way, how fast he had to drive, or how many corners he had to cut, everything would come up roses, just as long as he kept to the beat – an approach to life he could never explain to Brünhilda, who hated to be hurried and was a dawdler by nature. However, his belief was going to be sorely tested before the day was out, for Fate had decreed it. Beside him, turned away, curled into a foetal position, Brünhilda with a pillow pulled over her head.

In the kitchen, the lightshade, dangling the knotty pine that lined the ceiling, trembled, and Mickey's eyelids twitched as, three floors above, the dead-mans weight descended and the turret bedroom's hatch lifted. There came the clatter of leather-soled slippers descending the stairs.

Then the door to the hall flew back and the kitchen flooded with light as the toggle bead of the roller blind snapped up against the window frame. Through the vagaries of Victorian glass, the postman's red van driving off, the panes vibrating as a lorry filled with pink gravel from the quarry rolled past the head of the drive.

'Come on ya bastard, move. We've a load to pick up today!' Wolfgang shouted at the recumbent form stretched out before the Aga cooker. Then, getting no response, he kicked the underside of the bench. Unbelievably, Mickey began to snore.

ROACH HERE ...

Novgorod, September 12th, by the Volkhov River.

Wolfgang was forever warning about the danger of hubris. 'Never congratulate yourself too loudly in case the fates are listening and the next card out of the pack is a spade.'

Well, Wolfgang sure drew the Ace of Shovels in that Bogota Hotel room (see appendices – Emereldas). So much for his vaunted knowledge of the hidden aspects of life. But then Wolfgang rarely practiced what he preached, preferring to leave that to others in his employ.

But the Laird is dead, long live the Laird. I'm to have that unoriginal epitaph carved above his tomb. That is, if his body is ever returned by the Italian customs authorities, who have it in a deep freeze in Genoa after a sizeable quantity of cocaine was discovered sewn into his stomach, where presumably it had been placed by the Colombian morticians. Which is ironic, because he much preferred hash.

Today I received a further instruction via the Kingdom Consul. I'm to commission a new mausoleum, the grander and more castellated the better. Somehow I don't think so. Even supposing his book sales pick up, I hardly think the royalties would even cover the cost of drawing up the plans, far less the cost of construction. Mind you, should the film rights be sold, that just might prove sufficiently remunerative, of course only after the executor's fees are paid off. But a cockroach's wants are small. Just a few crumbs to cover my expenses, that's all. Who knows if those Italian customs officials hold onto his body long enough and sales finally pick up. Wolfgang might make it for his permanent lying-in-state.

tombstone with a view

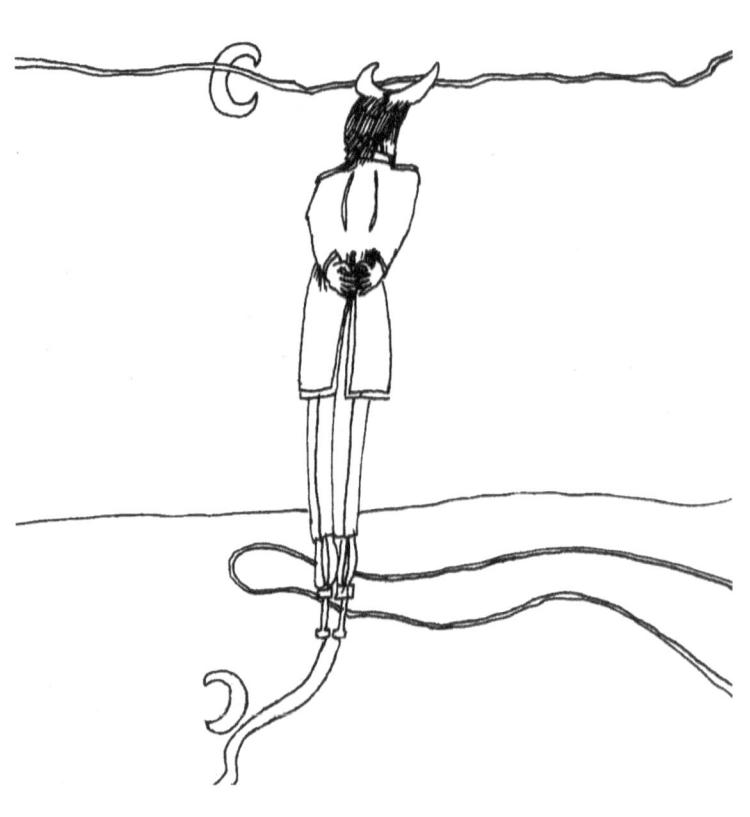

ON THIN ICE

Herman Dudley Wallinghope

In Brünhilda's misfiring Riley salon car, Wolfgang and Mickey were lost. Nothing new in that, they'd always been lost, but this time they were really lost, their informant's directions to the derelict factory complex and promised plunder, two mere hanks of wool in stoned minds unwinding, as all afternoon, towing an empty trailer, they rethreaded and rethreaded the maze of back roads of the Kingdom's Black Quarter. All around, blistering ruin, the plain dotted with slag heaps, some smoking from underground fires still burning after two hundred years. Wormcasts, pyramids and clinker fortresses, topped by scaffolds, gibbets and wheels of abandoned pit workings silhouetted against the leaden sky, which bore down like an up-turned bowl of porridge it felt so heavy.

Scratchings of the monster of progress' first passing, Wolfgang mused, for wasn't this plain where that black spore had landed and, finding fecund ground, had divided and divided again, and the world's first industrial age was born. The legend of Prometheus and Pandora, come around again. Another a gift from the heretic god who brought us fire, and a box which once opened could not be closed.

Less than 200 years later, the resources of the planet were two thirds consumed, and yet cuckoo technology's appetite was still growing exponentially.

Mickey McFinn wasn't interested in Wolfgang's speculations, the world, populated as it was by shit-heads, could be consumed by fire next week for all he cared. He was far more interested in the joint he was rolling with Wolfgang's lump of Nepalese hash – black as the wasteland universe, black as the boredom of this pointless journey. Mickey knew Wolfgang well, in his book there was no quicker way of getting to know someone than working side-by-side on a building site. Work that, it must be said, had to be fitted between Mickey's smack binges and enforced absences when the cops were actively looking for him again. When he returned, he'd perform the unlikeliest feats before the lads – his estwing hammer flashing in the sun. That's how Wolfgang would always remember it, Mickey spinning on the worn heels of his cowboy boots, snatching the falling hammer from behind his back. Then, at piece time, between onion bridies and mince pies still hot from the bakers in Snaresburgh, beating all comers in marathon press-up contests. Mickey reaching hitherto unattained maximums, his pale face turning purple, the veins on his neck taut as guy ropes, always jumping to his feet in a grandstand finish.

Mickey would do anything for the buzz of adrenalin, like when he leapt onto the blade of a bulldozer as it passed at full speed. Or for a side-bet, in the pub when work that day was over, bloodying a fist punching a three-inch nail into the counter. But when it came to work – regular sustained work – he had to be cajoled, dragged, threatened, blackmailed, and off, more than on, when Mickey had haunted building sites in Germany, this is how they'd been at it, since Wolfgang started his 'renovations'.

The knowledge they had gained of each other in their on/off relation-ship was double-edged, a coin if tossed would always land heads-up, the other face ending up in the dirt. That was the way it had always been, all their countless lives past, Mickey and Wolfgang, brothers in all but name, looping their sun – Brünhilda as she was presently called – in mutually opposed orbit, though they knew it not.

Yes, Mickey knew fine well, it would be hours yet before Wolfgang would submit and throw in the trowel. Even then, since this was designated a trip for plunder (Wolfgang's words) they'd have to pillage something, if only a garden gnome, just so's he could march into the kitchen of the big house and hold it up to Brünhilda, like the conquering hero he most definitely was not.

Wolfgang was the most contrary, most pig-headed, obstinate, obscure-minded bastard Mickey had ever known. Never any point telling him anything. All you could do was watch his lairdship digging himself deeper into his choice of doo-doo that particular day. But for all Wolfgang had been born with a fucking silver spoon, come dummy tit in his gob, thirty years and not yet weened, he had the biggest wind-up of his life coming, as sure as Mickey was a McFinn.

'Listen, Mickey.' Wolfgang broke the silence between them, a black brew brimming with unvoiced thoughts – a mind suck blanking-out the sputtering of the vintage car's misfiring cylinders – even the squeaking of the empty trailer bumping on the potholes of the narrow road behind. 'Why don't you make an effort to navigate instead of rolling another joint with my nep? I know I said I'd include it in the expenses till your debt is paid off, but there's got to be limits, and that nep is supposed to last us till after the weekend.'

'Aye, youz and the company store. I didnae hae tae offer tae pay it oaff...'

'Don't give me that shit, Mickey. Sometimes it's more work to get you to work, than any work you do, you know that!'

'A fuckin' man needs his smoke. Aye, 'specially if I'm tae stay oaff the booze...'

'And the rest,' Wolfgang interjected.

'Aye, an' the rest.' Mickey paused, stumbling on the words. 'Moanin' bastard. It's youz that drives me tae it, dae ye ken that? Aye, an fer yer information, cunt, the Kingdom's flooded wi' that nep.'

'What's up with you, Mickey? All afternoon in a warm car, well at least it is now, since you mended the heater. Thanks, by the way. Chauffeur-driven, my company...'

'I could hae warned youz it'd turn oot a complete waste o' time.'

'So why didn't you, Mickey?'

'Youz ask me that, Christ!' Mickey couldn't come up with the right words.

Changing the subject, Wolfgang pointed to an approaching tentacle of the town ahead. The backyards of the miners' cottages, strung out with washing drab and colourless as the town itself. Weeny front gardens, filled with crap – so many bedpans held out for Matron's inspection in a hospital for intestinal diseases.

'Look,' he said, is that really Cowpatten *again?* I don't believe it. How many times and how many angles, those same dead streets. Do all roads in the Kingdom lead here?'

Wolfgang noted a large tractor in the road ahead advancing on them like medieval siege machinery, clots of manure plopping onto the narrow road from the sharp prongs of its raised muck rake.

'Damn this Kingdom' he cursed, pulling into the side of the road, making way for the tractor. 'Always four roads to every place. Much as I hate to stop, I'll just have to ask the way at one of those cottages.'

Just as he said 'ask', Wolfgang noticed the registration plate of the tractor was 'ASK 23'. Simultaneously, black feathers fluttered, as a large crow swooped low and fast before the tractor as it passed and settled on the porch of the nearest cottage, over a dull green door. No. 23, daubed in red, in large crude numerals by a childish hand.

By this, Wolfgang's home-grown belief system, which was predicated on coincidences, had been renewed. For if GOD was not chance what was the motivating force of the universe?

Wolfgang didn't even bother with the wooden gate, which anyway looked to be in a state of collapse. Instead he vaulted the picket fence and delivered a salesman's rat-tat-tat knock on the old door, the lower edges of which were brown and desiccated, suggesting it was consumed by worm and rot.

After a long minute, during which he made out the ticking of an old clock, came dragging steps. Then the door rattled as bolts were pulled. Against the protests of rusting hinges, the door was drawn back to the mean limits of its guard chain, presenting a slice of crab-apple pie, and a red-rimmed eye, in which Wolfgang perceived, or thought he did, the flaring of slow dying embers.

'An' whit be ye wantin'?' came a harsh voice that put him in mind of an old 78 rpm record, the scratch across it extracting an involuntary shiver.

'I'm looking for the old Kingdom brickworks, ma'am,' he replied, grimacing at the smell of cabbage and carbolic wafting from the dark interior of the hovel.

Slowly, a pale shank of arm extended through the gap in the door, the arm's wrinkled skin twisting the opposite way to the elbow bone as the hag's claw hand settled on the eventual direction.

'Gang past the crossroads,' she croaked. 'A-a-aye, then tak the firrrst left turrn, past Kingsknowe orr ye'll miss it. The gate's mark'it by twa tall stane obelisks, like they had in Auld Egypt only they werr built by the masons o' the Kingdom. Ye'll see them in th' br'ak in th' trees. Tha's the whaur the auld brick wurrks wuz, but ye'll be wastin' yer time. A' the Wurrks is the noo is a muckle smokin' black hole in the grroond.'

'Ah, that must be it, there. The entrance to hell, heh heh, by the looks of it!' Wolfgang laughed as he did when anything appealed to his sense of dramatic or bizarre, pointing to a pair of leaning obelisks positioned to either side of a rutted track, in a gap between the roadside poplar trees. He could make out nothing beyond except a mass of yellowish fumes.

The fumes were from subterranean fires, he realized, smelling sulphur in the air as he drove the car between the tall, blackened obelisks. Beyond them, the ground was smooth, no more ruts, potholes, or puddles. Gone was the track, and it was all track ... nothing to do, but drive on into the embrace of rolling black slag and yellow plumes. They were in a foreign county, for no such landscape existed on any of Wolfgang's maps of the Kingdom.

Stopping the car and opening his door, Wolfgang reached below the Riley's running boards.

He was commenting on the warmth of the ground and the glutinous, even consistency of the dirt to Mickey, silent all this time, sitting in the passenger seat, when Wolfgang noticed a tall, trim, slim man in a suit so black and sleek it looked to be made of neoprene. He was stood still as a pillar, on a nearby rise. On his arm ... surely not. Wolfgang's heart skipped a beat, momentarily seeing the man and bird as a Rosenbach inkblot carved out of void, instead of just outlined against the leaden sky.

'Mickey, do you see what I am seeing?' he said, out of the corner of his mouth. 'Is that really *Him*?'

Supremely indifferent to their approach, the stranger stood as though commanding a high pass, which the pilgrims must climb to reach the celestial city in the hinterlands beyond – at least that's what Wolfgang imagined, hurrying ahead of Mickey who, unusually, was lagging behind.

The man's aquiline profile turned away in disinterest. His saturnine face furrowed, yet smooth. A translucence there, a wash of blue, the pellucidity of mortician's marble. His smile, all-knowing, cynical. Hooded eyes, Prussian blue in dark summoning. Hair, cropped steel, yet within serried ranks incipient satyr curls forming.

As they approached, the crow perched on the man's arm cawed loudly. Wolfgang noticed the bird's feathers had the same soft sheen as the cloth of the stranger's black suit.

For the second time that day Wolfgang shivered.

The man, if man he was, could have been almost any age from thirty-five up. Finally, he turned his head their way, arching a brow.

Scrambling up the slope, Wolfgang had the weird thought that the curious squeaking underfoot - compacting wet shale, he knew - was a multitude of tiny voices crying for restitution, as if the Kingdom Works had reduced its workers to microbial slag by the processes invoked in early industrial Satanic rites, and here was their master, returned in full flesh, surveying his pits of short bloom and eternal destruction.

How now brown cow, surely not the correct way to address the devil. *How do you address the Devil?* Wolfgang pondered, for the stoned part of his mind had indeed recognised that this was the 'Ill Ane' as He is called in the auld tongue of the Kingdom.

Mickey, coming up behind, was spooked by the electric discharge he sensed in the air around them. He was cold despite the heat underfoot, goosebumps breaking out under the shirt he'd borrowed from Wolfgang that morning. All he could think was to get somewhere else ... and fast. Instinct, however, bid him not to turn his back in case he offended spooky fucker ...

Wolfgang then dove into a rapid rendition of all the weird coincidences - only the most significant of which, for brevity's sake, are herein included - that had led him to this most desolate of black spots in the Kingdom.

Throughout Wolfgang's wordy exposition on the workings of 'chance' the stranger listened attentively, his eyes all the while on his domain. After Wolfgang had finished came a silence.

Then the stranger said, 'When ye'r staundin' agin' a gale, wi yer feet oan shiftin' saunds, it's best tae be mindfu' life's nowt mair than a passin' bedrock o' fictions.'

Unable to accept this terse reply was all he'd managed to elicit, Wolfgang probed a finger towards the stranger's familiar - the bird. Ignoring the blood that welled on the finger where the crow pecked it, Wolfgang then asked, 'D'you keep crows, sir?'

'Aye, them and dogs.' He nodded, an alabaster finger stroking night wing feathers. 'This wan haes a broken wing that's healing.' A chuckle formed in a waxen larynx. 'If ye'r lookin' fer the Kingdom Brickwurrks, they wuz turned tae dust ages past.' The stranger smiled. 'Ye'd be lookin' fer buildin' materials?'

Sensing Mickey's uneasiness behind him, Wolfgang nodded. There had been no mention of anything concerning their search.

The stranger turned and pointed. 'Gang in yon direction an' ye'll soon find the path, aye an' mind yer footing. It leads past a trickle o' water that was once a fast flowin' river. Cross the burn whar the fence bridges it an' ye'll find yersel's in the backyard o' Auld Jock McClaarty, deals in a' manner o' junk, a scoundrel o' sorts, but no the kind tae fleece ye's.' He chuckled, glancing down at Wolfgang's legs. 'Nae doubt ye'll find whit yer looking fer there.' He raised a finger, 'But mind no tae tell him A' sent ye's, otherwise he'll be sure nae tae deal wi' ye ...'

The stranger, the Man, had been as good as his *wurrd*, for in auld Jock McClarty's yard they found what Wolfgang was seeking.

The long-sought stained-glass window for the stairwell in the big house, mahogany handrails, balustrades and perfect wooden beams for a balcony to span the width of the great hall, all at a most reasonable price – after some haggling, of course. And there would be more, lots more, from auld Jock, who to Wolfgang was the embodiment of Moses – hands which could have parted the Nile *and* held back Ramses' chariots. Over a grey bushy beard that would not have disgraced the prophet were grey blue eyes that were still clear despite his age. Wolfgang guessed from his war stories that had to be his eighties, although it seemed impossible from his vigour and obvious strength. Recognised by all who dealt with him as the king of demolition merchants, what auld Jock didn't have in his yard *wasnae* worth mentioning.

The sky was darkening when Wolfgang and Mickey, replenished by sandwiches and tea provided by Jock's two wives, set off back across the black pits, promising to return in ten with the trailer for their first load. For once Mickey walked ahead, his one thought to get the car first and the lump of nep stashed in the old Riley's glove compartment.

Wolfgang, however, was hanging back, scanning the ground, looking for something. He didn't know what. Attentive as ever to the voice of his spymaster in his head, he was playing that old game which had often turned up trumps, resulting in all sorts of finds in odd places over the years. Never anywhere as odd as the black pits, he thought. Fucking Lucifer – as if. He was trying to remember which of the humps was the one where they'd talked, all of them looking much the same. Wolfgang guessed the Man must have been a miner, living in Cowpatten, out for an afternoon wander with his pet crow when they bumped into him –

Yes, that was the rise where they'd conversed, he was sure. Something anomalous on the very spot where the man had stood, he saw, as he clambered up the slope. The object looked to be a stone.

On closer examination it was a very odd stone, like no other Wolfgang had seen. Radiating heat, it lay heavy in his hand as he rolled it one way on his open palm and then another. On one side he perceived the disdainful profile of the Stranger, on the other, the snout and teeth of the black dog of his nightmares.

Fuck it, there was even a sharp protuberance, like the beak of a crow.

As he rolled the stone over to see it better, the fucking thing pricked his hand - second time that day. Seeing a spot of blood on his palm, Wolfgang knew he was in very great trouble indeed. What was he supposed to do with it? This dog devil stone was dangerous he knew, but he couldn't just walk away. Finders weren't just keepers, they were responsible, that was the un-written law. Perhaps it was a message, by asteroid post from the alien spy master, who now was silent. Nothing coming through in his head, when he needed answers most of all. It proved you couldn't rely on anyone, not even inner voices, he thought sourly, forgetting many great finds in the past. Fuck, he needed a spliff to work this out.

Though all the woes which followed him thereafter, at least Wolfgang found solace whenever he returned to that demolition yard for more building materials.

Often invited for the night, he'd be entertained by Auld Jock, who'd delve into his kit bag of old tunes, playing his fiddle fingers that seemed impossibly large, dancing on the strings, his other hand bowing so fast it blurred. His wife, Dotty, a big grin on her soft face, rattling her skiffle washboard, keeping the beat, over on the settee in the corner. Beryl, his other wife, standing between them, hands on ample hips, her head tossed back, belting out the words. By her bare feet, Hector, the ancient Alsatian dog, splayed out on the hearth rug. Wolfgang was never able to work out which wife was No. 1 and who was No. 2, as he sat drinking whisky before a blazing fire of scrap wood. in the bungalow.

He had a view of a plastic wishing well on a square of astro turf, walled in by towering scrap that screened out the pylons of the adjacent electricity sub-station. Much of the scrap was chrome: grills, headlights, hubs, bumpers with fins, and panels of 50's American cars, the shiny metal mixed in with stacks of tyres, long wood beams, fenceposts bound up in tangles of wire ripped up from small farmsteads, at that time in the Kingdom being bulldozed to make way for new housing estates.

The big pig outside, was named after a Nazi that Auld Jock, then a Sargent Major, had captured in his castle in the Black Forest.

'An aufie nice man, wi' a muckle snout, and fat as yon auld porker,' he said, pointing through the picture window at Goering the gross pig over by the plastic well, happily munching on trash spilling from a heap of bank sacks that had fallen from the wall.

Auld Jock was a mean fiddler, and one of the Kingdom's greatest characters. It was rumoured that during the last battle of WW2 he'd played with the Devil in his castle and won a great prize, though what it was no one could say. Some guessed it might have been the devil's pipe.

cutting the stone

with stone.

CUTTING THE STONE WITH STONE
by Harvey Woodstock

Everything is dark in the castle, except for a light burning in the top floor studio of the East Tower, where a laird has fallen asleep contemplating the devil stone. He nodded off sometime around midnight.

For a spit-second, opening his eyes, Wolfgang is back in the black pits, staring at the saturnine face of the man in black. But no, he realizes, it's only the devil stone on the desk, by his head. He knows it a meteorite now, having compared it with photos in a book on meteorites from the library, after testing it with a strong magnet that is still stuck on, indicating a most powerful magnetic field. He supposes it sheered off one of the icy planetesimals of the Oort Cloud he fell asleep reading about, at the very limits of the solar system, before hurtling to Earth. But wherever in the universe it originated, the damned thing is now his responsibility because stupidly he picked it up. What to do with it, that is the riddle he must now solve.

But instead, his mind drifts back to the conversation with Mickey in the car, after their encounter with the man in black. Any other time he would have found it hilarious, but not as it got dark on the drive back to the castle.

'You don't know what it's like,' Mickey whined, 'always chaffin' ...'

'What the fuck are you on about now?' Wolfgang, who had been miles away, snarled.

'Youz telt me if ever I needed to talk tae tell youz. It ain't just all you middle-class cunts who hae feelings they dinnae ken whit tae dae wi ...'

'What's the problem then, Mickey?'

'I telt youz a' ready, it's my dick.'

'What about it?'

'It's the size o' it.'

Wolfgang laughed. 'Is it too small then, Mickey?'

'The opposite, it's a good 6 inches too big.'

'How's that a problem?' Wolfgang grinned.

'You've nae fucking idea, man, when I walk, what wi a' the chaffin' o' my troosers, a' the blood rushes down tae my gonads, an' then a' ah can think aboot is gittin' relief.'

'Why don't you wear a kilt then, hang loose and free? That's your solution, Mickey. I'll lend you one from my collection – that is,' he added, sourly, 'unless Brünhilda's given them away to her favourite charity while we've been away.'

'Can ye see me in a fucking kilt oan a buildin' site? Besides, kilts 're for posh cunts like youz. You'd never catch me in wan.'

'I am trying hard to take you seriously,' Wolfgang said, grinning.

Mickey shook his head. 'Nae one ever understands wha' it's like. I thought at least you'd be different ...'

'Well, explain then,' Wolfgang said, impatiently drumming fingers on the steering wheel, 'I'm listening.'

Mickey sighed. 'Nae troosers ever fit, and wimmen're alwuz lookin' at it bulgin' in ma jeans.'

'And that's a problem?'

'Weell it can be efter they see it.'

'Uh huh.' Wolfgang nodded. 'Go on.'

'Well first they gasp, and their face goes red as they realize their friends werenae exaggeratin'.' He shrugged, responding to Wolfgang's incredulous look. 'Oh, sure once I hae finally worked it in, they like it right enough, between a' their shrieks and cries. But then efter a few times stuffing them like Christmas turkeys, they've had mair than enough shaggin', and then you get the usual excuses. It's nae fun I tell youz, that's why I take the smack ye ken and get pissed. I'm never able to hud on tae ony woman, 'cause it's tae fuckin' big.'

'You are serious?'

'What, d'yew think I wud fuckin' lie aboot somethin' like that?'

'I don't know.'

'Fuck's sake, Wolfgang, dinnae let me down noo. Cannae youz understaund, I'm desperate.'

'I would have thought you might see it as god's gift and not a problem.'

Mickey sighed, 'I thought at least youz wud understaund.' He turned away and, staring out the car window, ended the strange conversation.

Perhaps he had dreamed it, Wolfgang wondered, but no, he had often seen the bulge in Mickey's jeans, like a rubber tube hanging down the inside of a leg, halfway to his knees. Everyone had, though it was never discussed by the workers - at least not within his earshot.

WOLFGANG'S WORD BLOCK
by Victor Steppenwolf

Za-Za stopped typing for the 'nth time that morning and regarded the putative Laird severely.

'Ok.' Wolfgang shrugged. 'So that was not up to my usual standard. Another line would help.'

'Wolfgang, you are already owing me for three this morning.'

'You know I'm good for porridge.'

'That is not the point.'

'Well what is then?'

'While I don't mind typing whatever verbiage comes out of your mouth, I can't stand stopping and starting as you've been doing this morning.' She pointed to the wastepaper basket, which was filled with scrunched-up balls of paper. 'It's usually just three words before I have to start again.'

'This next passage is exceptionally emotionally difficult.'

'Perhaps you should come back to it later. Or better still, skip it all together.'

'But we're getting to the crutch, er, I mean the crux of the story.'

'Wolfgang, by now any reader, should you ever acquire any, will have worked out what's going to happen between Brünhilda and this so-called Mickey Mcfinn.'

'But it was so traumatic, especially after the analogy of stuffing Christmas turkeys in the context of him shagging my wife.'

'For you personally, Wolfgang, but you wouldn't be the first laird to be cuckolded by one of his serfs.'

'You think so?'

'Yes, that happens all the time on the *great* estates.'

'Doesn't make it right.' Wolfgang scowled.

'At last the laird revealed a prude!' Za-Za slapped her knees. 'For your information, and you can quote me in your goddamn book if you ever get it published, Skull has walked in on me more than once.'

'With who?'

'*Whom.* His pals?' Za-Za shrugged. 'I don't know.'

'What did he do?'

'Nothing, he is not possessive that way.'

'I find that difficult to believe.'

'It's true, one time he even sat in and watched us, before I knew he was there. It's not a problem with him like it seems to be for you. But then he's not a prude as you are, Wolfie.'

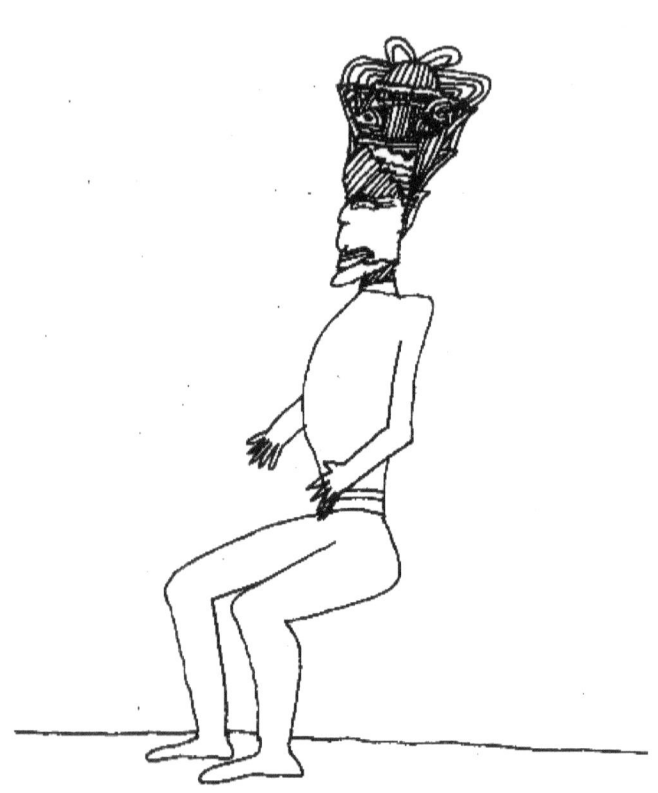

WAITING FOR MOVEMENT
by Swami Harri Raj

Within a picket fence once rampant with sweet peas and honeysuckle, sadly withered since Brünhilda had departed the fold, stood a small chapel-like building which Wolfgang had seen fit to construct after a mind-expanding retreat in an Indian ashram some years before.

Outside, the walls were whitewashed for purity and inset with tiny mirrors to repel the evil eye. Even the number of steps leading up to the wooden door, ingeniously carved with the lingham of Shiva, were ritually important for, as Wolfgang's swami had taught him, three is the number of Man – body, soul and spirit.

Inside, the room was mostly devoid of features. An old windup gramophone had been placed in a corner, and two low foot-shaped plinths, were positioned either side of a hole in the stone floor, which descended into the bowels at the back of the building.

Presently, Wolfgang was taking time off his word block, his feet on the plinths, squatting with his trousers about his ankles, listening to a scratchy 78 RPM recording, issuing imposing brass horn from the antique wind-up gramophone. The record was a favourite from the old Laird's collection, a command performance of Tannhäuser by Richard Wagner before an invited audience of Nazi dignitaries in the *Bayreuth Festspielhaus* opera house circa 1938. Wolfgang usually found it inspirational, but less so that particular morning after his failure to describe the action between Brünhilda and Mickey in the silver caravan, where he'd caught them inflagrante all that time ago. However, that said, the power of Wagner's music rarely failed to elicit a physical response from the Laird of Castle Haggard.

Just so today, when the overture climaxed, and Wolfgang felt a corresponding movement deep inside.

Breakfast lunch and tea, come and get it,' he yelled, as close below came a frantic snuffling from the resident plumbing system – the albino pig permanently quartered in the picket enclosure at the back of the loo.

Wolfgang was just about to let the pig, (always ravenous at that time, its head pushed, up the funnel-shaped hole as far as the snout would go, hot breath on his bared ass), have its first feed of the day, when the door protecting the sacred space crashed open. Silhouetted against glowering red clouds, Skull, blocking out the light, armoured in a metal-studded biker's jacket. The shoulders were shiny with rain, above padded lederhosen and clumping great riggers boots. He stood, pointing a finger at the Laird of Haggard, unfortunately caught with his pants down.

'*Je bent dood*, cunt face,' he yelled, as Wolfgang struggled to free his cock, caught in the zip of half-mast trousers.

'And what's brought this on?' Wolfgang managed to say, after a moment of liberating pain.

'*Bastaard* screwing my fucking woman.'

'Ah, excuse me!' Wolfgang said, standing up, finally zipping his trousers. 'Your woman she may be, but she's my secretary according to the terms of the contract we both signed, and which I understand you tore up.'

'*Ja*, that I did,' Skull growled.

'Well it's fortunate I kept a copy. For your information, I do not screw employees of either sex. And what may I ask is your reason for this unannounced visit?'

'Fuck, the vay you lords in this stupid country prattle in your *belachelijk kasteels!*'

'It's called having an education,' Wolfgang said, forgetting he possessed no educational qualifications whatsoever other than a certificate stating he had dyslexia. 'How can I help you?'

'*Ik haal je later wel in*, Lord Cunt! When you least expect it.' Skull turned and left the Goanese Loo as quickly as he had entered it, just as a loud explosion sounded from the quarry, which was followed by whooshing noise, then a dull crump, as another section of the Crags of Haggard Hill, slid from a cliff face, the impact of hundreds of tons of falling rock striking the ground on the other side of the railway embankment, shaking the foundations of the castle buildings, including those of the Goanese loo.

'Feeling better now?' Za-Za said, brightly, looking strangely cheerful as Wolfgang entered the conservatory.

'Fucking lucky to be alive after being assaulted in the loo by Skull,' he snarled, noticing a few more glass panes of the conservatory had been cracked by the blast from the quarry.

'He said you were quite rude. Anyway, you don't seem to have any injuries.'

'None you can see. He's defiled the loo, which was a sacred space. I doubt I'll ever feel peace in there again. The pig's still to get his breakfast and will probably have to wait all day now that my sphincter's seized up.'

'Diddums,' Za-za pouted. 'Poor Wolfie, it must have been a shocking experience.'

'It was.' Wolfgang nodded, easing into his chair. 'And he thinks I'm sleeping with you. I wonder where he got that idea from?'

'Really?' Za-Za looked surprised. 'I said nothing to give him that impression. Perhaps he's just jealous of you being the laird.' She waved a hand at the dripping black stones of the east tower. 'And of this, uh, fine, uh, mostly renovated castle.'

'That's probably it.' Wolfgang scowled.

'Care for a line, Wolfie?' Za-Za said, taking a glass vial freshly topped up with grey powder from her waist bag.

'Absolutely. Make it a double, I deserve it.'

A VISIT TO MAD HATS
by Grant Utterleigh

Though generally known as Kingsburgh, the proper name of the capital at the time of writing, was actually King Willburgh, HRH King Will the 3rd then being the Head of State. This was following the death of his father King Harold VII, who'd had a fatal seizure during the ceremonial proroguing of Parliament the year before.

The change of the name of the Capital, was the source of much gainful employment for the Guild of Cartographers, because Article XVI of the Constitution required that all maps of the Kingdom had to be reissued with the updated name every time a new monarch ascended to the throne. Not that that was a problem for the citizenry, who went on calling their capital Kingsburgh, as they had always done.

The capital was world-famous for its annual International Narcissism Festival, which was held in the ancient network of abandoned passages and sewers under the Old Town. All that was known about the tunnels' origin was that they predated the mediaeval Old Town of Kingsburgh by perhaps as much as two millennia, though that was a matter of dispute among experts of the Department of Archaeology at the University of Kingsburgh. Even their extent was unknown, though the main passages under the Old Town itself had been surveyed by the guild of Cartographers, and tourists visiting the underground city were provided with free maps that marked out safe areas such as the Hilarity Quarter, outlined in green. Every few years attempts would be made to flush out the homeless resident in nooks and crannies and the criminal enterprises of denizens in deeper levels, but these always failed, mainly because the city derived considerable income from fleecing the tourists who were encouraged to explore their every deviation in the vaults below the busy streets.

By the means of a cunning conduit that bypassed the S&M Quarter in the Fetish district, where all year round dominatrixes plied a busy trade, and for a moderate fee tourists were whipped, wrapped in clingfilm, and hung from hooks for as long as they liked in the groined vaults, Wolfgang arrived at the residence of his old mate, and the downtrodden woman who had the misfortune to be his wife, in the old drugs quarter.

As usual it was Morag who opened the door, below the psychedelic neon sign on the wall above, that flickered *Mad Hat's*.

She was obviously dressed to go out, wearing animal print tights that left nothing to the imagination on her skinny legs, a pink mohair top, a gold navel ring on her bared midriff, and Cleopatra purple eye make-up not applied thick enough to conceal a fading yellow bruise around one eye.

She motioned over her shoulder, with a red-varnished thumbnail. 'Your timing's good as usual, Wolfie, he's just lit another one. Sorry to miss you and all that, but I cannae stay. Bye.' And with that she was off, down the corridor, red stilettos that matched her nail varnish clicking around the next corner of the dimly lit labyrinth.

Inside, the vaulted octagonal dealing room was decorated in the manner of an Indian temple. Its recessed stone walls were hung with garishly coloured fabrics printed with Urdu script, and the eight niches around the room had shiny images of Hindu deities whose doe eyes belied their fearsome postures.

Occupying a throne-like gilt chair in the middle of the room, clad in a Sai-Baba T-shirt and orange pasha pants, his long brown hair pulled back in a ponytail and as per usual wreathed in blue smoke, Bungalow Bill grinned behind his Zapata moustache as Wolfgang entered. The heavy metal door, propelled by an automatic mechanism, clanged shut.

'Bom Shankar!' Bill boomed – not in greeting, as Wolfgang knew from experience, but in invocation of one of the multi-armed zoomorphic deities looming in from the niches around.

'Boom Shankar yourself,' Wolfgang replied, accepting the cone-shaped joint that Bill held out for him, before sitting down and crossing his paws best he could on one of three monstrous cushions, all the seating available.

'I'll hae tae trade that wun in fer a mair recent model.' Bill nodded in the direction Morag had just left. 'The day I married her the wind changed, moanin' cunt. Never stops complainin' despite a' the skag I gie her.'

'Is that so?' Wolfgang dissembled, mindful of the oath of silence Morag had extracted the last time he dropped by on the off-chance, and found her kissing a Bill lookalike, outside the same door by which he had recently entered. Leastwise, he speculated, a lookalike to how Bill must have looked about two hundred thousand joints and forty thousand chillums ago.

Secure in the knowledge he was the unchallenged biggest prick in the Drugs Quarter, and apparently oblivious to the fact that his wife was trapesing through the ancient sewers to a secret assignation with her lover as she did every Wednesday at this time, Bill reached into a cool box at the side of his throne and tossed Wolfgang a can of local brew he got from the crate out of the back door of one of the many breweries in the Old Town of Kingsburgh.

White froth fringing his drooping moustache, Bill lounged back in his throne, his lock-jaw grin expansive as ever, though just occasionally, as Wolfgang knew well, the grin slipped, and he would say something that was not loaded, or sneering, but sharp and pointed all the same.

'Hey.' Bill sat up. 'You still cuttin' aboot wi' that broad frae the States – ye ken, the one wi' the electronic conkers.'

Wolfgang laughed, couldn't help himself. 'I take it you are referring to a Yankee baggage possessed of perfect double yolkers.'

'The same.'

'And how did you come by this information?' Wolfgang demanded.

'Ocht Wolf, some things ye cannae keep tae yersel', especially that one, you and me being good mates an' a' that.' Arching a brow, nearly bushy as his moustache, he leaned forwards on his throne. 'C'mon ya cunt, gie uz her number and tell her I'm hooked intae a big spike deal. That should bring her runnin'.' Bill wiped the froth from his moustache with the back of a hand. 'Here, are ye's goin' tae smoke that hale joint a' by yersel'?'

Accepting the joint back, Bill took a deep puff. 'No a bad smoke eh? Plenty mair if ye'r wantin' ony ...?' he paused, then, getting no reaction from Wolfgang, continued, 'Well are ye goin' tae put my proposition tae her?'

'I suppose I might, even though I don't think she'd be interested.' Wolfgang shrugged. 'That is *if* the baggage ever turns up again on my little bramble patch,' he added, again reminding himself of the state of veg garden.

'Ho ho, an' it's no so little! Christ ye've don a'right fer ye'rsel' o'er the years. But tak a wurrd o' advice.' Bill's grin slipped meaningfully. 'Sweeten up that wumman o' yours, an' smartish, o' ye'll loose the lot. The wurrrd is, she's been oot clubbin' at the Sawney Bean wi' that dike sister o' yours.

'Step-sister, you mean,' Wolfgang said, his eyes narrowing at the implications of this latest titbit.

'Whitever.' Bill shrugged. 'The point I'm makin' here is, she was yewrs fer life, gift wrapped 'n' served oan a golden plate. Ye must hae dun sum'thin terrible, an' nae mistake, fer her tae leave ye's.'

'We're just having a break, that's all, *bogart*,' Wolfgang said, in a sudden swipe snatching the joint from between Bill's fingers.

'Aye right!' Bill laughed. 'So whit are you wantin' the day? I've some crackin' pollen I guarantee ye'll like.'

'Actually I've still got some of that boring leb left you sold me last week.'

'Ocht this pollen is fuckin' way better. Naebody in the toon kens dope as well as me, but nae bastard'll believe me when I tell them it is Afgani, because it looks like Moroccan.'

'That's because your legendary reputation always precedes you.' Wolfgang laughed.

'Heh, heh. An' ye ken why that is?'

'No ... oo.' Wolfgang shook his head, enjoying the banter which was distracting him from the unwelcome news that Brünhilda had been clubbing with the sister he called *the Thug*.

''That's because I'm alwize wan step a-heid o' the pack.'

'You mean one step above them,' Wolfgang chuckled. 'And your prices are too high.'

Bill sat back, a pained expression momentarily replacing his slice of cheese. 'Come-oan Wolf, noo-a-days every Tom, Sick-boy, Judas Cunt and Harriet's at it. Why in this passage alane, I've lost coont o' the hustlers. An' it's no just hash, weed, coke, scag and' a bit o' speed, like it used tae be. Noo-a-days, it's downers, crack, nembys, gee-gees, head-sacs, dizzy, spike, acid, and what's the new wan called?' he snapped his fingers for the name, lost it. 'Crazy designer shit from Sicily, a hun'red times stronger than the grade A heroin thae doctors dole oot tae OAP's thae canne fix, in yon geriatric hospital up oan Moont Pleasant. Imagine that!' Dumbfounded, he shook his head. 'How lang dae ye think the wurld's got when even Paki corner shops 're sellin' glue kits under the coonter tae kids barely yet weaned? It's nae right, ye've got tae draw the line sum'whaur. Sum'wun should shop them tae the polis ...'

'I wouldn't mind some acid,' Wolfgang said wistfully, 'haven't tripped for years.'

Bill brightened. 'I've a bag o' tabs here, by my chair. Listen, if yew buy that ounce, I'll sling in a tab for free.'

'Nothing's free with you, Bill,' Wolfgang snapped, calculating he could always sell the pollen at a profit if it wasn't to his refined taste. 'Make it four tabs and I'll take it. But if the pollen's underweight or the acid's no good, you know I'll bring it straight back.'

Bill threw up his hands. 'Christ in a' my days, I've never met onywun sae tight as yew, Wolf. Yew're a fucking Scrooge.'

Wolfgang shook his head. 'It's just that I take a page out of your book when I come to visit.' He grinned. 'Too long in the tooth where you're concerned. Now,' he continued, in the same sharp tone, 'Is this acid really any good?'

Bill's eyebrows, which were almost as bushy as his moustache, shot up. 'Green star and crescent, the best there is, all the wie frae thae fucking Jihadist towel heids, ower in Kalifatia.'

FREEDOM IS USING A KEY
by John Lockhart

A horrible suspicion having formed in his mind after his recent conversation, seeking anonymity from caller display, Wolfgang pulled up and parked the Riley by one of the last remaining phone boxes in Kingsburgh, conveniently near the parental home. Inserting the correct change, he keyed in the familiar number, hoping to catch the Thug, who still lived there despite earning good money, having qualified as therapist some years earlier.

Instead, his stepmother answered.

After exchanging the usual unpleasantries, Wolfgang asked the question most pressing on his mind.

'Is by any chance Brünhilda there?'

'As a matter of fact, she is,' his step-mother replied, coldly.

'So,' Wolfgang said, heavily, 'am I to take it she's staying with you?'

'Yes, I've given her your old room.'

'I see.' Wolfgang's knuckles whitened on the phone receiver. 'Can I speak with her please?'

'No.' His stepmother's tone was final.

'Why not?' Wolfgang glared into the middle distance outside the phone box.

'You ask that, after the way you have treated her. She's told me all about it. And I must say I think you have behaved disgracefully.'

'She's my wife. You have no right to come between us.'

'Wolfgang you are a brute and a bully, and I have every right to protect my poor abused daughter in-law.' And with that, his stepmother ended the call.

'Fuck.' Wolfgang stared at the receiver in his hand, which in his rage he had ripped from the coin box. 'Fuck fuck fuck.' He slammed it down repeatedly as, with a disengaged part of his mind, he realized this was the same phone box he'd vandalized when he was seven by ripping out an identical receiver. Then, a familiar throaty roar alerting him, he looked up just in time to see Brünhilda behind the wheel of *his* Lamborghini, driving past at speed.

'Fuck me!' he swore, stepping into the middle of the street, watching as the Lamborghini careered around the next corner and disappeared in a haze of exhaust smoke. He didn't have a chance of catching her in the sputtering Riley, which anyway was about out of petrol, meaning he'd have to get out the spare five-gallon container he kept in the boot.

Hearing a familiar tapping of a cane approaching from behind, Wolfgang turned and was plunged into the vortex of a dream, forgotten until then, from the night before. For there, coming along the pavement, shuffles his father, these days almost completely blind from glaucoma. The semicircular scar where the thyroid was cut from his throat was concealed behind by a carefully cultivated long grey beard, which he strokes when pontificating. In his shabby brown mac draped like a cloak over his back, and with his permanent stoop as he leans on his cane, catching his breath, worried the next might be his last, he looks more like Methuselah than whatever biblical patriarch he imagines he best represents.

'Wolfgang, is that you?' He stands pathetically, reaching out a claw hand. Finding his son's shoulder, he grips it, bearing down with hydraulic pressure as if his fingers were steel instead of just gristle and bone. Smiling grimly as any skull behind his beard, the old man says, 'Shoulders straight, boy,' his exhalation dislodging some crumbs from the stained whiskers around his mouth. 'That's better. Now chin up, Remember to do your duty. Now, go back. Go back to the castle, and do your duty by your wife.'

Fuck that shit, and fuck that crumby beard the old wanker hides behind, Wolfgang thinks, vowing never to grow one. Without a word, he turns and walks away.

Round the next corner he stops, remembering more details from his dream. Yes, there were stars, and a white dog, and sure enough when he looks up there it is, the white dog sitting on the sill in a high window by a polished astrolabe, the brass glinting in the late afternoon sun, dappling the upper floors of the stone tenement across the tree-lined street.

Dreams within dreams. Parallel realities open up. Vertigo, a sudden feeling of falling, as he sees different versions of himself trapped in a maze of forking paths. Tinker tailor soldier sailor, rich man, beggar man, thief. Which ghost is him? Were they all him?

Wolfgang comes to with a start. He realizes there is no doggie in that window, and there is only one iteration of him looking for it. Nor is there any dog sitting in the other windows of the tenement opposite.

Perhaps he had imagined it? Was he two sheets to the wind, off his rocker, stressed past Neptune to the Oort belt with five years of refurbishing Castle Haggard and doing his duty by his wife *and* his scarred, scared old man?

With another start, he notices a girl pushing a pram along on the opposite pavement in the direction of the nearby park. Their eyes meet, she smiles, he smiles, and Wolfgang sees that half her face is scarred by a purple welt, which she could have masked with cremes and face powder but obviously hadn't, clearly not giving a tuppenny damn for any one's opinion. She is simply beautiful. Regal as Queen Boadicea's face on a two-guinea gold coin of the realm, a coin never withdrawn from circulation. It was an oversight of the Treasury in the 17th century, during a crisis that paralyzed the small nation's economy, and legend has it the coin was rarely even seen.

Turning to watch her go, pushing her pram, Wolfgang feels brushed by gold dust wafting at her passing, and knows she just saved his soul.

Looking up, he notices the white dog is back in the window next to the astrolabe. So he didn't imagine seeing the brass ornament either. He realizes then all of it is a dream ... but whose dream exactly, since he's in it. Or is he? Is it a composite view? From the angles and perspectives of his scattered selves – who for all he knew co-existed in parallel dimensions where paths forked and time ran contrary, or in poorly ventilated brain compartments, drip-fed by neurons, putting up with power outages during the not infrequent brainstorms – it was hard to get his head around ...

ANGEL DROPPINGS

This poor guardian angel, the burden of my responsibility, a dragging chain, making manoeuvring amid the flocks of cirrus in the heavens, none-too-easy.

I see it all from here, you know. Old Methuselah scratching out his sentence below (Methuselah is gnomic, i.e. of the lower earth – all mortals have this aspect). And on the next rung of existence, Wolfgang. Such a worrisome fellow with his beastly inclinations and transgressive legs. Ever since he was a zygote, when at his conception I was assigned to his case, I can't help but see things through his eyes. Against my better judgement, I am forever whispering advice in his ear, but he's so fogged-up with the various vicious substances he will insist on imbibing that on those rare occasions when I do manage a penetration the truculent fellow pays no heed. And when he takes lysergic acid? My! The promethean current shorting his astral chord turns these wingtips quite electric blue. Gloria in Excelsis! Pax maxima! And that's not nice I assure you. For despite what some lesser divines would have you believe, it's not all fun up here, far from it. Wolfgang the tail that wags this dog, as a mortal might say.

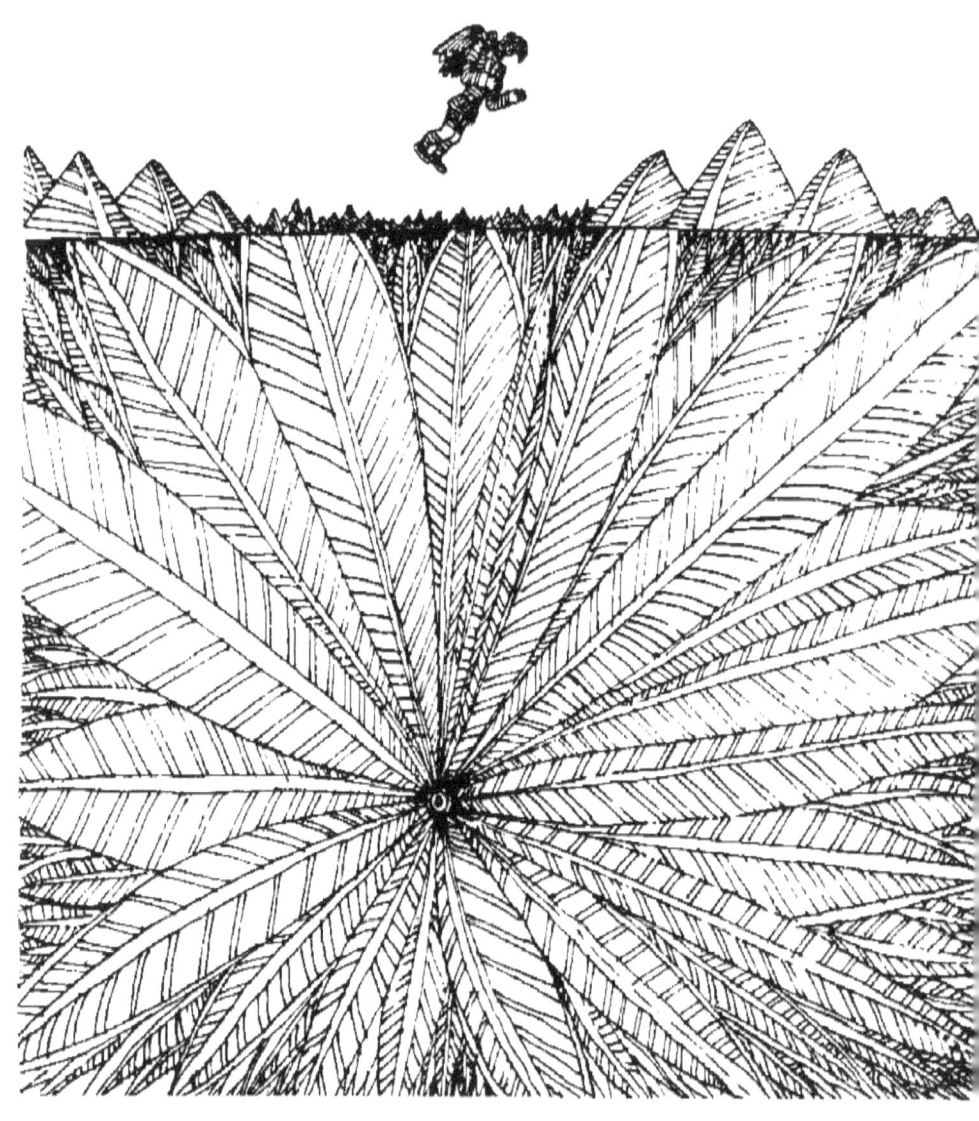

THE TRIP
by Victor Steppenwolf

A world away ... a world below, Mercury skinny-dipping in the long valley's shadowed depths, where the river serpent whispered into its patchwork bed of rumpled fields, sharing the secrets of Nile, Danube, Limpopo, Volga, Mississippi, Dnieper, in its straights and meanders... Blue to battleship grey ... rust-grimed grey ... In the sky, driving down from the north and polar regions, winter's heralds, foreclosing on autumn's sale, grey-bearded outriders, gap-toothed, foul-mouthed dragons all, trumpeting time, their hoary breaths, backcombing a zillion origami scales on the shivering pelt of ...

A laird on walkabout on Mourning Rock Hill...? Surely not ...?

Re-orientating desperately, Wolfgang, or whoever he was, transferred his gaze onto hands held palm down, fingers splayed, raw knuckles meat red, tributaries and deltas where blood corpuscles circulated under translucent skin.

Wrapping arms, *his* arms, he realised, Wolfgang became aware how cold it was ... How cold he **was ... how cold his unbearable armour of flesh was**
...

'H ... h ... ome, g ... o ... t ... to g ... et ... t... home ...' Wolfgang spoke aloud, or tried to with a jaw that seemed primitive ... unused for 10,000 years and so, so very unfamiliar. Perhaps he'd stepped back in time and home was a cave. Lying in wait in its smoky depths, lickably stretched-out on animal pelts, woman, wild and unfettered, gnawing on a charred bison leg that would always, if required, double as a club.

Some things never changed.

Fading Neanderthal senses had warned him. Regression had indeed traded his castle for a cave, hot and choking with smoke, yes, and Goldibollocks grown monstrous in the vast intervening time, reclining on purloined cushions in the kitchen of the big house, her normally pale Siberian countenance ruddy to the rafters of her eyebrows from several electric heaters ranged in audience around, the Aga stove having gone out, rosy cheeks nestled into the fur of Brünhilda's great-great grandmama's sable coat. Between her fingers, a cigarette supported an inch-high column of ash that, to Wolfgang in his present state, seemed to tower over him.

'Well look a-here, it's the wild dishevelled Laird of Haggard!' For his cave-coming, Za-Za had assumed a Louisiana State Penitentiary drawl, 'Whatever have you been up to, Wolfie? Or is it McMoses down from Mount Horeb after crawling into a burning bush with George?'

'Please, don't talk so loud ...' he whispered, hoarsely, 'been tripping all day.' Dropping to his haunches, Wolfgang pulled a heater about and began rubbing his hands back into existence.

'YOU GOT ACID?'

Za-Za's feet slammed the boards to either side of his lowered head. Those startling sapphire eyes, looming huge before his face as snapping fingers demanded, 'Me want, me need, me must have. GIMMIE!' And when he just stared back, stupefied by close proximity and her unwashed vixen scent, *louder*, 'WOLFGANG, DON'T DARE PREVARICATE. I have just spent two of the most damnable days of my entire EXISTENCE ...!'

'SHUT UP!' Wolfgang shouted, 'I don't want to hear another word about it ...' Then, remembering he was supposed to be coming down, and not flying into a lycanthropic rage, he hunched lower. 'Look,' he said, weakly, 'I have just managed to spend eight hours without trauma of any kind. Which, considering my potential for psychosis ... is an IMMENSE ACHIEVEMENT. But now ... again ...' he panted, 'you're spoiling everything!'

'Wolfie, you're holding out on me. Every one of my sick senses tells me. I won't take any excuses.' She held out an outsize hand, palm upwards. 'SO GIMMIE, NOW!'

'Oh alright!' he snapped. 'Anything to buy peace. It's there.' He pointed. 'Tucked behind the curtain rail on the left side, and there's only two tabs, so restrain your guzzling maw. DO YOU HEAR ME?'

'I read you, Wolf brother.' She was there already, one foot on the windowsill, the other precariously positioned on a tilting chair-back. 'Ah, we have it,' she breathed. 'Shit! Am I really seeing this?' Inhaling a freight train, she stepped down. 'Kalifatia supertabs?' A bruised eyebrow shot up. 'Wolfie, you've really scored this time. I heard this latest batch is lightyears ahead of the sadly never-to-be-no-more Hammer and Sickles ... and, though I hate to admit it, I never did think much of Stars and Bars tabs, goddamn CIA no-goods.'

Reaching out, taking hold of his fist, she prised his bunched fingers apart.

Wolfgang stared down at the star and crescent tab courtesy of the Kalifatia High Command glowing green on his palm. A beacon? He wondered. Maybe it was and at that moment secret agents of the Fundament Front were sneaking in the vegetable garden outside and the Jihad was upon ...?

'Now take your medicine like a good bow wowsie and leesten to the story that mummy has to tell you...' She held up an index finger that looked to be at least a couple of meters high. 'One, two...'

Lulled by the saccharin coating of her southern drawl, closing his eyes he beheld – after an absence of nigh-on 30 years – how he had mourned – the face of his long-lost mother as she leaned over his cot to deliver a goodnight kiss. He had been such a good pup the whole day and this was his special treat.

'THREE!'

Obediently he opened wide and, as she popped the tab into his mouth, again he savoured the tang of spearmint on his tongue. Nice touch, he thought, Kalifatia High Command had to have been getting marketing assistance from somewhere. Coca-Cola? Possibly, since they were into everything oral, nasal and alimentary.

Then, with a jolt that shifted several thoracic vertebrae, Wolfgang realized, too late, he'd just ingested another eight hours of Eternity into his head. A long and wearisome road, stretching to purgatory, overhung roiling red and black clouds that reminded him of his duchess's undergarments, which she wore on Sundays in memory of her mother, who still haunted her.

Turning, he noticed with alarm that one of the strings stretched across the maps on the kitchen wall was pulsing the same colours from where a paper flag was pinned...

'Wolfie?'

'Shut up!' he growled. 'I am trying to remember something,' he added, instantly forgetting what he had just seen.

'Cannot you eeeven handle vun leetle treep.' That voice, now Ruskie-accented, was getting closer. The rogue KGB closing in ... 'Ve haff vays to make you ...'

'Definitely and most certainly not!' he snarled.

'You are haffing to leesten anyway.' The Commissar turned brusque. 'You are haffing no choice! And now if you are ready leetle children. Ve shall begin. Yesterday it vas, no ... I call it ze day before. Just after the cum-oozing Skull vent AWOL, I am discovering he ees only stealing my passport, and zer ozzer papers zat prove to ze whole world I am me. I looks in ze meeror, and I am no longer zere. But to get away from me, leetle cheel-dren, eet ees not zo eezy, and in chicken pox hours, heh heh, I track heem to hees lair, the Snaresburgh Yachting Club hut, from vere he has been spying on uz ...'

'Za-Za, please ... talk normal,' Wolfgang protested, his eyes still screwed tight shut, hands over his head.

'I almost had him,' she said, her accent slipping. 'Do you know I actually had my passport and his wad, all of his money, the whole fucking twenty grand of it, in my hand, but then his sidekick Charlie the Rat crept up on me, like this...'

Wolfgang cracked open his eyelids just in time to see Za-Za springing up from all fours, her green claws reaching for his throat.

Stumbling backwards he collided into an electric heater, toppling it over. The element flashed blue as the castle's lights fused, pitching him into a darkness instantly greater than the grey twilight outside.

'Wow, that is the most unbelievable, most incredible ...' he muttered, staring at slowly fading electric bars. Reaching behind his back, his fingers touched the chair behind him. He sat down, just managing to connect with the edge of the seat. 'I'm getting the most amazing blue after-flash, like Bird of Paradise feathers ... no, like angel feathers.'

'Wolfie!'

'Really, really amazing. This acid is amazing.' Then, hedging his bets in case any Fundament Frontists were hiding in the weeds outside the kitchen window, still on his knees, raising his hands, he declaimed, 'Praise be to Allah ... er um, Za-Za, tell me, how does the Muslim call to prayer go?'

'Wolfgang!!'

'Yes dear, I am listening.'

'I need your help.'

'What, me?' His eyes widened. 'In this condition ... Why?'

'Skull's been hanging out at Menace's. He's got my passport and ...'

'So?'

'I want you to help me retrieve them.'

'No! Absolutely not ... I refuse ... NO! NO! NO!'

'Wolfie, darling, my life is in danger. Don't you care?'

'Za-Za, you are more than capable at handling yourself. Honestly, in a survival situation, presently I'd just be a liability ... And besides, you're right. I DON'T CARE!!'

'You really don't care?' she pouted. 'Not even a weeny weeny bit?'

Castle Haggard possessed a demonic twin in the next glen, which though a faux castle only dating from the late 19th century was marked with a little flag, marking its importance on Wolfgang's montage of maps, because it had been built on the site of an ancient Pictish necropolis after which it took its name. The acquisition of Cadboll Castle, however, proved to be the absolute peak of Menace's achievements for thereafter the career of that wheeling drugs-dealing robber-turned-cattle-baron took a steep slide. A few months back to the considerable relief of most of those acquainted with him, Menace had been sentenced to seven years on a conspiracy rap.

While the cat is away, the mice are free to play, that hoary old saying never more true than following Menace's incarceration. All of his *sojiers* and sidekicks, rats to a man, descended on his castle. The prize herd of Aberdeen angus cattle, with which he had hoped to gain respectability among the landed gentry by entering them at agricultural shows, all died of malnutrition after overwintering in bare fields, and his wolfhounds had been removed by the Society for the Protection of Animals. Only his faithful steed, his wife Molly, the parrot in its cage, which was called Supergrass, a couple of cats, and of course, the vermin remained. Of these, the most noteworthy were: Charlie the rat, previously mentioned, the factotum who it was rumoured had an enormous scrotum, in charge of the drug mules; Skull, who had handled the Dutch end of the business; and Saxon, who had been with Menace from the beginning, when he started out as a humble poacher, gaffing salmon in the local rivers.

Wolfgang had a history with this demonic duo, having employed them during the drainage phase of the renovations, when Saxon laboured and

Menace leaned on his spade and looked on, telling jokes and laughing at his sidekick, invariably deep in a hole, only the top of his head visible as he shovelled out dirt. Still it had been a worthwhile arrangement from Wolfgang's point of view, because when it came to earthmoving Saxon was the equal of a bulldozer, which cost a lot more to hire, or indeed a JCB, if digging a trench or a pit for a septic tank was required.

However their arrangement came to an abrupt end when Wolfgang discovered that Menace was smuggling drugs into the country via Snaresburgh Yacht club and had stashed three sacks of black afgani hash in the east tower, which he gleefully confiscated. But unfortunately, Menace then climbed in an upper window of the tower and reclaimed the heavy bags, lowering them one by one by a rope to Saxon, waiting in the darkness below. Thereafter barred from the castle, sometimes at night Menace would park his car across the entrance, peep the horn, and then when he was sure Wolfgang was watching, piss on the stone gatepost.

But then Menace bought Cadboll Castle in the next glen, and what had been a passing irritation to Wolfgang became a permanent annoyance, which was only made worse after Menace departed the scene and his *sojiers*, drug mules, and former lieutenants descended on Cadboll and took up residence in its many rooms.

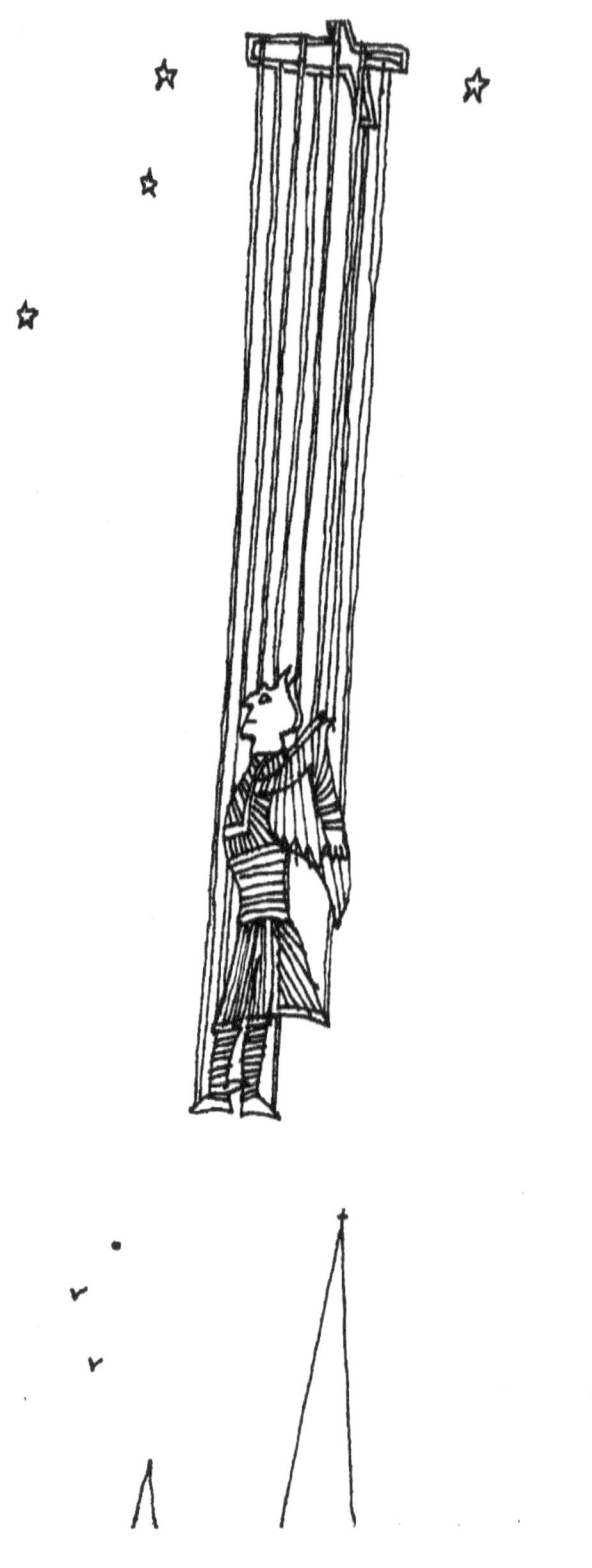

THE ANGEL AGAIN

There is such a scattering of carelessness to this life, so many combinations with which to frame events. Take this tin heap, about which Wolfgang's forever moaning due to its sputtering engine and colossal consumption of fuel. He says he can't understand it. Plenty of signs as to the cause, the omnipresent smell, the trail of drips wherever he goes.

He does notice such things, so there is hope, but ever faithful to his transgressive nature, he files the information away in a brain compartment that is blocked-off, rendering access impossible, except when events have moved on and it's too late.

Right now that petrol's dripping direct onto the vintage car's exhaust pipe, which in the normal run of things, as the motor heats up, might well prove a lethal combination, except that as so often before Wolfgang's multiple error system is working again.

Let me explain: the last time he tinkered with the engine, Wolfgang failed to reconnect two vital bolts, so the same jarring collision with the roadside boulder which punctured the fuel tank also caused the exhaust to separate from the manifold, hence the fuel drips onto a pipe that is cold rather than hot, as it otherwise would be. All this contributes more flesh to the bones of Wolfgang's modus operandi, a reversal of Murphy's Law, the principal of which is, simply get enough things to go wrong, then inevitably as night follows day, the most important things will come right of their own accord – no effort involved.

Proceed then with a maniac's intensity through life, as Wolfgang does, laying down the causal first links as you go, dragging the resulting chains and your angel skidding the pylons, why then the apples of Providence of their own volition will simply fall at your feet or, in Wolfgang's case, paws.

Yes, sounds crazy, but trouble is – don't ask me how, I certainly never gave him a clue – Wolfgang has stumbled on an actual working principal of the Universe. I told you he is a transgressive deviant. If only it were possible, I would have cleared my wings of him several mortal lifetimes ago, but I'm forced to hang here amid these broken harp strings and watch, as has been pre-ordained. Until he changes, no tune on my harp can I play. No tool can sever that chord and our connection. I wonder what it was, my crime, that I should have to serve out my sentence with this fool.

STEALTH IN THE NIGHT
by Hector D. Doublethwaite

Wolfgang shook his head determinedly, but it was no use, the purple spots bouncing a potpourri before his eyes simply wouldn't go away. But then he reminded himself he was tripping, and some purple hazing of his brain was to be expected.

VROOM ... for once no spluttering from the V8 engine, the vintage Riley was fairly flying, the tarmacadam rushing between Wolfgang's paws precariously positioned to either side of the gaping hole in the rusting floor, as the treadless tyres of the old car laid the road low.

VROOM ... at the railway bridge turn, another down shift through the gears, double declutching, forth to second, third absent, when was it not?

Wolfgang grinned as he succeeded with a trick which had caught many a hitchhiker by surprise. A combination of mounting G-forces and the bolts of the passenger seat having no grip on the rusting floor. Woops and over Za-Za goes, tipped over onto the back seat, whoopee, legs kicking in the air, a fine view of her arse in the rear-view mirror.

Something had to give. It could have been anything, Wolfgang supposed philosophically, springs, wiring, or whatever caused that smell of burning rubber whenever he drove the vintage car, but this time, unbelievably it was fuel, and he was so sure he had topped the tank off from the spare can kept in the boot, before they had set off.

Wolfgang and Za-Za sat without talking for a long time in the old Riley, the car having stopped where it had run out of fuel at the side of the road, just staring out at the oncoming clouds – no, not clouds ... far more scary! Slinkily came the grey moose, spreading its great antlers across the darkening blue, as it stooped to graze on the north-facing slopes of Mourning Rock

Hill, twilight creeping on Loch Duich below, till its still deep waters were nowt but a smear of silver in the claws of night.

Leaving the car, they trudged onwards, ever onwards, two weary pilgrims slowly progressing into the dark forest leading to the Valley of the Shadow. John Bunion never had it so hard, Wolfgang reflected, limping along, a Cuban heel missing from his made-to-measure cowboy boots, lost in a primeval swamp somewhere a thousand miles behind them.

When at last they emerged from a confusion of snarling roots, snagging branches, and voids for every second step that had been the dark forest – it was the first occasion they had held hands, he was to recall with great fondness later. Before them, in the depths of the narrow glen, Cadboll Castle seemed to be floating on mist. Lights on in its twin towers, one yolk yellow, the other lime green, two mismatched eyes of some alien beast, sparks flaring from a high chimney, a gust of wind carrying the sulphur smell of a slow-burning coal fire.

Standing at the head of a straight single-track estate road at the edge of the forest, peering into the darkness below, Wolfgang saw, or thought he did, strange ovoid luminous blobs flitting the castle's lawns. Impossible to make out what they might be. Meanwhile, at his side, Za-Za had assumed the form of an English setter dog, straining on her toes, pointing with her nose, snuffing the air.

On the lawn, two blobs came together, parted, and joined again, undulating rhythmically, as if dancing to an eldritch beat.

'Goddamnit! Wolfie, don't you see, it's a witches' sabbatt down there!'

This was a new Wolfgang, fired-up by her recent acceptance of his hand. 'Fucking-slime heads!' he roared, rocking back on his heels, laying down his challenge to the fiends of the night. 'Come and get us!'

Truth is stranger than fiction, this is actually what he did.

Then, as the last echo rolled off the slopes of the narrow glen, he was answered by a great bellow, that surely had been framed in the larynx of a deranged bull.

'UUUUYYYGGGAAAAGGGGHH... hooo ...ooo.' The animal roar which had started with such bullhorn force suddenly tailed off in a '...bloop ..de ...bloop,' sound, which Wolfgang's synesthesic senses perceived as a black tallow candle, as flame which first flared then guttered, before it was snatched by a djinn in a candy-coloured cotton sheet that came swooping down on the wind.

A third, central light had joined the others. Rectangular in shape, and actually a tall window, had Wolfgang been able to sort its constituent parts into a cohesive whole it would have afforded him a fine view of the castle's main staircase, and a monstrous silhouette rapidly descending the flights of red-carpeted stairs from one of the two towers above. Then, from the forecourt of the castle, a car's doors slammed, a powerful engine revved dementedly, before a wandering single light came on, slewing from one side of the road to the other.

This road, for Christ's sake, Wolfgang thought, this little bitty bit of pie crust my poor paws are planted on. Checking around for cover, he dismissed as inadequate the bare oaks of the long avenue of trees leading down to the castle.

'Come on, hurry!' he said, trying to haul Za-Za by the hand back towards the dark wall of the forest at the head of the estate road, a hundred yards behind them. 'Whoever's driving means to run us down.'

'That's exactly what Skull wants us to think, idiot!' she said, throwing off his arm. 'STAY WHERE YOU ARE!'

As they linked hands again, Wolfgang felt an inflow of strength, and this time, he resolved, he wasn't going to let go. Shoulder to shoulder they stood in the middle of that estate road which ran straight down past the castle and up the hill beyond, threading the narrow glen ... well, perhaps his shoulder was a fraction behind hers ... but solidarity, nonetheless, as that loco monster raced towards them, trailing sparks, a runaway train coming so fast it was melting the rails, its lone headlight a deranged cyclopean eye.

The runaway loco stopped, not one inch to spare, Wolfgang realized from a disembodied perspective, looking down on himself and at its cowcatcher out front, bumping his knees.

A moment's panic when he couldn't locate Za-Za, but then he saw her at the side of the cyclopean machine, hate and fury rampaging, kneeing the car's buckling paintwork, seeking to claw, batter, smash and sink her claws into the enigmatic black shape behind tinted glass. She'd have torn the door off its hinges had she gotten a grip.

With the whine of an electric motor, the driver's window of this recently registered, already half-trashed BMW slid down. The thinnest of swooshing sounds as a slimy gob landed on Za-Za's face.

All Wolfgang could make out of Skull was the billiard ball shine of his pate and the radiance of his ghastly grin in the dark cab as he slapped away the outsize hands reaching through the window, grasping for his throat.

'FUCKINCUMEATINGPIECEODUTCHSHIT!' She yelled, verbally profligate as ever, tossing back her mane, depositing more coins of unspendable rage into the bank of black night.

But then Skull leaned out, grabbed her topknot and hauled her, head and shoulders, into the cab, and sprang the trap of the automatic window.

Wolfgang rose from the ditch, where he'd been forced to leap when the BMW drove at him. But then it was slewing gravel, at the head of the road by the dark forest, and this time as it came at him again he had no Za-Za at his side to save him. Even though he hadn't put it into thought the first time, he'd known Skull would never run her down, but on his lonesome, it was a different matter entirely.

Pinioned like a rabbit in the glare of that careering, cyclopean eye, Wolfgang might have remained standing frozen in the road had not a picture from a history book sprung to mind. If the stratagem had been good enough for a King, he reasoned, surely it was good for a Laird.

Lying full length, hugging the long tree limb overhanging the road, it was quite a cameo Wolfgang beheld through the car's open sun roof as the BMW passed below. Skull was driving, one hand on the steering wheel, with the other gripping the nape of Za-Za's neck, forcing her head down... on a monster boner? Making a laird's penis piccolo by comparison, but no, he realized, it was only the barrel of a rifle propped between his thighs. Next to him, laughing his rodent head off in the passenger seat, Charlie the Rat.

Screaming up through the revs, the car shot by, Za-Za's feet, one of them missing a shoe, kicking futilely, like frogs' legs out of the window.

Good Bye, my amanuensis,
Who could stick a name on you,
The last of the gringo Inuits,
One gulp by the black Skull
And you were gone, gone gone,
Leaving poor Wolfgang on his ownsome
Still tripping and so-o-ho forlorn.

Silently, trying not to laugh at his last sight of a legs 11 Venus snapped in the jaws of a black clam, Wolfgang slipped from the branch, dropped to the ground, and leaned back against the broad trunk of the oak tree, needing the support because of the weakness in his knees.

With a chill that registered absolute zero on his spinal barometer, he felt a sinister emanation from the next sentinel in line of the long avenue. And what a tree, its great girth pregnant with a cancerous bolus split by a witch's grin, which sprouted wicker like a Strool Peter man plugged into the mains. That would have been bad enough, but behind the cover of frissoned shoots, a highlight glinted on the sharp edge of a blade.

As Wolfgang stared, a good half of that witchy bolus broke seal, and a ghastly, naked hulk, a pumpkin with yellow pigtails, supplanting shoulders that also supported a felling axe – the haft incongruously decorated with feathers – daintily stepped into the middle of the road. And stood, back turned, unknowingly sharing with Wolfgang the vision of the black meteor shooting past the castle on up the hill road.

Idly now, a fat hand passed down a glistening back, slipped underneath a loin cloth of a coiled sheet – all the apparel he was wearing. It picked some gunk from between thunderous buttocks, rolled it between sausage fingers, sniffed and flicked the nastiness aside. Then, as the taillights flared over the crest of the far hill, the dejection of Atlas seemed to fall on the axe-man. Hanging his head, he began plodding down the road towards the castle.

Asking himself if any of this was real and watching him go, Wolfgang tried to blink the axe-man out of existence, but it was no use. Yes, of course he knew this pumpkin, so lugubriously hefting the axe of his mental warpath. Unmistakably this was Saxon, last seen running into the distance, waving arms, shouting some froth about cunts, rape, and promising slaughter that never happened, if for no other reason than Saxon was a simpleton – the dupe who over a decade had made Menace a fortune backpacking dope over mountains, across international borders by passing the customs posts, and was now lost without him. The poor dupe, belatedly raging the hundreds of *thoosands of poons* he had made Menace, only ever rewarded with a slap-up meal and a bubble bath in a brothel, and sometimes not even that.

But this clearly was a different Saxon, his muscled bulk coated with a covering of lard, shouldering an axe decorated with bloodied feathers.

Had the world gone entirely mad, Wolfgang asked himself. Were scenes like this playing out in the next valley? And the next, in fractal scenes, across the Kingdom? Goddamn first time he takes acid in ten years, and this absurd reality wraps him in smutty silk excreted by a curtain spider.

The whole charade had the hallmarks of something pre-arranged for his personal derangement – the gods conspiring against him, when were they not ... evil Olympians, surveying him from their etheric palaces. Perpetually interfering in the lives of mortal men, relaying the results live on pay-per-view universal broadband for the edification of immortals across the galaxy. But what the hell, he considered, why not tag along with the masquerade, for the time being at least ... See what happens. All of it perfectly safe, just so long as he kept reminding himself none of it was actually real...

A wicked grin replaced Saxon's dolorous grimace, when like a sneaky cork Wolfgang bobbed up beside him and asked, 'The night is yet young, Lard Man, whither go'est thou with that feathered axe in thy hands?'

Wondering whether he had just said this, Wolfgang decided he had.

'Oi go to Scarborough Fair, sir, to meet the young maid who oi know is there, and I'm not lard man, Oi'm Pie Man, you've heard of me, surely?'

'I have, Master Pie Man, if that be'est thy name. But what will thee do if thou discoverest the maid's a cow, for most of them are, or didn'st thou know?'

'Then Oi'll cut off her horns, that Oi will do.' The brute licked his lips with a salty tongue thick as a butchers block. 'But oi'll leave the tail, sire, t'would not do to put tails in pies now would it, sire?'

'Uh huh,' Wolfgang muttered, non-commitally. This trip was getting weirder by the second. Maybe this brute wasn't Saxon at all. Again taking the initiative he asked, 'Been choppin' wood, hast thou?'

'No... oo.'

A fat thumb, cushioned as an arse on a smaller man, stroked the axe blade.

'All mornin' oi been sharpenin' it.'

'Indeed,' Wolfgang countered, regarding the thumb pressed on the edge. 'I always knew you were tough, but not that tough, surely?'

'I am that...' Saxon grinned idiotically, his fake accent slipping. Flexing a bicep, he faced Wolfgang. 'Feel this,' he said, through gritted teeth, presenting a bulging bicep.

Tentatively, Wolfgang touched Saxon's elbow. 'Shall I squeeze here?' he said, standing on his tiptoes, peering up into Saxon's eyes to determine what sort of dope the moron was on. No, it wasn't dope, he concluded.

'Up a bit and roond,' Saxon gasped, gritting his teeth.

'Here?' Wolfgang enquired.

'No, higher.'

Gripping biceps massive as a bison's, barely making an impression with his fingernails, Wolfgang made as if awestruck. 'MAN THAT IS HARD!'

Underneath his coating of lard, Saxon had turned quite blue.

'Pweeeeuufff!' he subsided, an overinflated Michelin man encountering a tack.

'Now, you must tell me, dear.' Reaching up, Wolfgang patted Saxon's meat pie fondly, ruffling his yellow hair. 'What's this obsession with cows? Surely a nice boy like you doesn't need to go all the way to Scarborough Fair when there's plenty of udder udders around?'

Then, as puzzlement bloomed on the big dolt's face, Wolfgang chuckled. Then Saxon laughed too, the basso sound from his cavernous belly resonating with the mating call of a toad in the marshes beyond the avenue of old oak trees.

Companionably, this strange couple (one with furry legs, limping slightly on one paw, the pupils of his eyes as big as saucers, the other a man mountain, naked apart from the loin cloth about his waist and slathered in lard, a feathered felling axe slung on a shoulder broad as a barn), walked together down that road so dark, through the avenue of oak trees.

As they neared the tall ironwork gates, they found them lying half-open, leaning back against stone posts. The castle beyond was hooded in darkness, a lone shaft of light cresting the hill road at the head of the glen. Kapitain Von Kirk, searching for his lost monocle in space, Wolfgang thought disembodied, regarding the meteoric BMW clam descending the straight road towards the castle.

Revving dementedly, the BMW cut the gap between the staggered gates, sparks flailing, its undercarriage scraping the speed hump across the entrance, its exhaust muffler bouncing into the bushes to the side, the car slewing 360 degrees into the gravel forecourt, spraying the castle's windows, ta-ta-ta-ta-ping! And then 'ow—ow-ow' as the sharp stones of the rotating fusillade of gravel struck Wolfgang's hairy knees, protruding from the thick ivy on the castle's walls. From there, he watched the BMW's trail of havoc continuing along a section of trellis garden fence, splintered wood flying, the concertinaed trellis hanging like the sting of a scorpion over the craft as it finally ground to a halt by a battered Range Rover parked at a right angles to a Mercedes with four flat tyres, by Cadboll Castle's pillared portico.

Erupting the car holding the rifle, Skull ran headlong into the castle's portico, followed at a more sedate pace by Charlie the Rat, who emerged whistling from the passenger side of the BMW. Reaching the castle's open door, he looked round, checking right and left, but failed to see Wolfgang hiding in the ivy, nor Saxon and his axe concealed behind a pillar on the other side of the portico. Still whistling his tune, which Wolfgang recognised was 'The End' by The Doors, from the movie Apocalypse Now, he disappeared inside, leaving the castle's door half-open, orange light from the entrance hall fantailling across the forecourt, silhouetting weeds like a sieging army of rats – come the impending Day of Judgement, this castle would be theirs.

It took a full minute before Wolfgang worked out the muffled bangs and yells were coming from the BMW's boot.

He was Za-Za's friend, wasn't he? Well yes, but perhaps, he reasoned, thinking clearly for the first time that night, it might be better for all concerned if she remained where she was.

'Let me out ... let me out ...' If anything the volume was increasing. He supposed something must be done. However, on first inspection, the catch of the dented boot proved inoperable. Wolfgang then waved Saxon over and pointed to the problem.

Obedient to the laird from the next castle, who at least temporarily, had replaced Menace as his master, Saxon bent down, hooked his sausage fingers into the impacted offside edge of the back of the car, and with a grunt heaved the boot from its hinges.

So much for Vorsprung Durch Technic, and progress through technology, Wolfgang thought, getting his German car models mixed up as, with an idle toss, Saxon sent the boot spinning into a tall topiary bush which, though unclipped since the inception of Menace's regime, was still recognisable as a toucan.

Za-Za emerged from the boot, the pupils of her eyes wide as the black lagoon. But it was her hair which chiefly alarmed Wolfgang. God, it was matted with blood ...

Replay that, he thought, not liking that detail one little bit ...

... matted with engine oil, from a squashed canister revealed below her flanks, as, like a jack-in the box, she sprang out of the boot. Inuit genes he guessed, small spaces no problem after millennia confined in their igloos, the cold never a problem of course.

'Wolfgang, my hero, my saviour!' She was about to embrace the laird – wrapping arms and legs – and reward him with a kiss worth five buckets of porridge, when she noticed Saxon shyly waiting in line for his share of the commendations.

''And what do you want, bright boy?' Za-Za snarled. 'The price has gone up since yesterday. It's now seventy-five pounds for a bubble bath and a rub down! Dirty-minded ape is too good a description for the likes of you.'

At the mention of bubble bath, Saxon started shuffling forwards.

'Take one step closer,' she yelled, pulling back an arm – Artemis the Huntress, drawing her bow – 'and you'll get this!'

His fantasies of being lathered and scrubbed by mummy's giant hands dashed again, Saxon brought juddering hams up to his face and, still ogling, began chewing his knuckles.

'ZEUSSSSS! The Huntress imprecated the heavens, raising oversized fists to the night sky, 'remove this slavering pig from my sight this *instant!'*

Shouting incoherently about cunts and rape, Saxon sped off round the castle walls, to the animal sheds at the back, another chicken to slay, as a Laird finally got his reward when Za-Za planted a smacker on his cheek. 'Wolfgang my *fwavourite pwotector* in the whole wide world *fwor ever!'* she pouted, hanging on his shoulder.

'Cut it out,' he snarled, pushing her away, getting his hands implicated in the process. Didn't she realize she was covered in oil? The viscous stuff, mineralized from plants that lived hundreds of millions years ago.

'You've got to help me with just one more thing ...'

Placing his palms to his ears, Wolfgang got them implicated too. *Christ,* he thought, imagining the black essence of carnivorous plants trickling down his ear canals, from a dark Eden roaming with ghastly dinosaurs like Skull.

'Goddamn it, Wolfie, will you listen to me?' She pointed. 'You've got to disable this car. If I don't recover my passport I'm lost. I've got to keep him in the castle till I've gotten it back, don't you see?'

What he saw were hands scrabbling in the black depths of the engine compartment. *His* hands, he realized, leaning closer to watch them at work.

He had always admired the way mechanics went about their business, and those hands were no exception, busy as nit-picking crabs in the depths of a primeval lagoon flicking over stones in search of prey, only those were clips.

'There,' he said, pointing at the rotor arm in the exposed distributor. 'If you really want this alien craft disabled, you can remove that.' He straightened-up, brushing his hands professionally as he thought, *I've done enough*.

'But my favourite, favourite man,' Za-Za breathed, pressing close, 'It's such a little thing, are you positively sure it will disable the engine?'

Wolfgang, who had seen the operation performed in a movie, sighed, realizing he was going to have to explain the deeper mysteries. 'Za-Za, clearly you don't know *anything* about quantum mechanics.' Again he pointed. 'Look, the rotor arm there passes the charge to the ...'

'Well that disposes of *that*,' Za-Za said, as the distributor cap span off, rubber hoses extended like octopus tentacles disappearing into the stygian depths of the Sargasso sea. 'And now are you ready?' she said, slyly.

'Ready for wha-at?' Wolfgang asked, suspiciously, reminding himself once more that the woman was congenitally, terminally, pathologically insane – but more to the point, tripping.

'I told you already, *we've* got to get my passport. It's not in the car' – she nodded towards the portico of the castle – 'so he must have it inside someplace.' When he said nothing, she turned away, muttering, 'Goddamn creampuff soldier... '

'Try to be reasonable.' Wolfgang grabbed her arm. 'I can't handle much more of this. Please, come back to the castle with me. We'll be safe in the big house ... and warm ... I'll make you tea ...'

'SNIVELLINGGODDAMNCOWARDLYCONDOMSUCK-INGPUFFPASTRY!' Za-Za whirled back around. 'None of you goddamn pricks in this land has enough spunk to stand erect like a real man. One four-foot-two wetback Manuel with a glass eye entered in a Texan bull rodeo is a better bet than ten of you bums in this so-called Kingdom! All I want is a modicum of psychological cover. A MOD-I-CUM! You won't actually be called to do anything. You have my word. In there I know I am on my own. Now are you coming, or do I have to go by myself?'

Tripping the labyrinthal corridors of Cadboll Castle, into which for several years unlaundered drug money had been funnelled, sparing no excess. Sadly however, in the absence of its incarcerated laird, the designer wallpaper was now peeling in dripping recesses and framed pictures of Menace in bars, on yachts, up mountains, at international borders, high-fiving customs officials and standing at the prow of fast boats speeding between Tangier and Gibraltar lay broken on the damp carpeting which covered the original flagstones like invasive fungus.

An ill wind blew down the corridors, from behind doors hanging off their hinges and windows left open in deserted rooms. The draft lifting the tassels of repro medieval tapestries of bearded menaces in kilts tossing cabers and suchlike at the Kingdom games, of which Menace was a fan, and for which the country was universally famed. Not a shortage of spunk in them good old days, certainly. Wolfgang and Za-Za were forced to duck as they passed.

Corridors, more corridors, each with their designer theme – mock Tudor: the ceilings lowered and crossed with plastic fake wooden beams. Black Forest gateau: cuckoo clocks in the recesses above Teutonic suits of plastic armour propped against plaster-daubed walls. Psychedelic bungalow: matching carpeting and wallpaper, swirling with fluorescent colours, no need to trip, the effect was the same, the recesses fitted out like bar-room snugs with vinyl seating and built-in tables. Wyoming log cabin: log benches in log recesses hung with moose horns. Every third-rate motel from Two Egg in Florida to Slickpoo in Idaho, from Dirty Shorts in Texas to

Deadhorse in Alaska, taking in all styles – in other words Kingdom drugged gothic.

When they finally parted, she was back pressed against the red rococo flock wallpaper, neck craned, arms spread, fingers splayed against the wall, working her way up the marble staircase towards the upper floor.

Always that girl has such a great sense of the dramatic, Wolfgang thought, watching her doing the CIA shuffle, ascending step by step, till at last she disappeared behind the porphyry balustrades of the next landing, heading for the tower apartment above, where she had been bunking up. Yes, the girl was a double agent, had just confessed to playing it both ways, and hanging out at Cadboll Castle in her spare time when not gainfully employed at the Imperitor. But what the heck, his supply of golden oats was not inexhaustible and he could only afford to pay her so much porridge. Perhaps Skull really was waiting for her up there, as she suspected? He hoped so, and that they would come to a final resolution, one way or the other. For if these infernal distractions continued, it would constitute a breach of her conditions of employment, and he'd have no other recourse but to instruct Jaws to draw up a letter of dismissal and then look for another secretary.

But however events conspired, as events will do, his novel must go on, that was the main thing.

Now looking for a way out of the castle and its forking corridors, which were starting to remind him of the maze back at his castle, Wolfgang stood before a heavy door - one of several in the long passage. He was considering the light leaking under the door jam, painting the toes of his cowboy boots a lurid red and blue. Anything might be lurking behind the door's heavy oak panelling, he conjectured. But what the heck, he was a laird on a covert mission in enemy territory and would forfeit his remaining self respect if he turned away. Resolved as much as he could be, Wolfgang took hold of the repro Florentine door handle, featuring the head of Bacchus -brass, one of a thousand such handles shipped from Palermo in Sicily to Menace in the Kingdom, each one packed with an ounce of zentanyl, a designer drug 100x stronger than smack - and pushed the creaking door open to its furthest limits.

Sprawled in various poses, draped on sofas, chairs, and backs against the walls of the baronial room, the denizens of the castle. With the exception of Supergrass the parrot, which welcomed his appearance in the doorway with a desultory 'fuck me,' all of them were tuned into the zentanyl channel, playing in the dead zone of their heads. Beside the parrot's gilded perch in the middle of the room, cross-legged on a high bentwood chair like a fakir on the Ghats of Benares, one stick arm stuck in a vertical position above her slumped head, the queen of the castle, Menace's wife, commanding the denizens of Cadboll to rise up and give her head.

Perhaps they already had, Wolfgang considered , surveying the branding of the splayed carapaces - T-shirts with the nomenclature of a lost Kingdom generation ... *Party till you drop... Blow me... Head Doctor ... Dead on Arrival ... Cum Fry with me ... if you ain't driving that train who is? ... Monster Orgasm Donor ... HIV positive and proud ... Trans-am 80 genders mile high Club ... Fuck Babies ... Ham and Egos where I go ... It ain't gears Baby it's Devil's gristle*

... and, of course, the de rigueur skulls, razor wire roses, and Harley Davidsons which, in their condition, none of the assembled could have swung a leg onto, far less ridden.

The bodies were draped around the large room, red-lit from the overhead light bulb, blue-edged from a looping screen on the DVD upended on the floor in a corner ...

On the other side of the curtained room, sudden movement – Gollum eyes transmitting but not receiving. Mickey, resistant even to zentanyl it seemed, syringe in shaking fingers, the needle sliding into a worm vein, his discoloured teeth drawing tight the leather belt binding his arm, its brass buckle biting into his pale skin ...

Watching him slump as the drug took effect, a memory replayed in Wolfgang's mind, from when they were best, or was it *worst* friends, *before* Mickey stuffed Brünhilda like a capon and everything went wrong.

Overhead, a million sparks spiralling into clear moonless night, flaming tongues voyaging among the stars, the constellations of the Milky Way whirling, as spinning they danced, melding Brünhilda's body to his. On the other side of the blazing fire, Mickey hunched over his drink, brooding dark eyes rimming his glass. Pretending not to look but looking all the same – the bead of his eye homing in through a torture of flames as, from the speakers, the chorus line repeated over and over...

> '*She's my worst friend's best girl,*
> *She's my best friend's worst girl ...*'

Shaken by a sudden spasm, Mickey's head jerked up, then slumped again, his chin striking his sternum. The tiny bubble of blood on the tip of the needle, a red apple falling ... a child's balloon, drifting free. Perhaps this time, he would get his wish, and not return.

So much to remember, so much to forget.

Wolfgang snarled as, kicking aside the insensible limbs of recumbent bodies, he crossed the room, set the DVD player upright, picked a disc at random from a slew of them scattered on the floor, and fed it into the slot. Pulling a cushion from under a shaven head tattooed with a swastika, he squatted down and prepared to be amused.

So tell me something new, which I don't know already, Wolfgang thought, leaning over to turn off the DVD player, and a SF movie about an evil band of Eternals who, finding a pristine planet on a spiral arm of the Milky Way, genetically manipulate a harmless species of vegetarian bipeds they find there into a compliant workforce. For sport, the Eternals, who like all of their kind suffer from terminal boredom, force the apes into gross acts of degradation, and even have sex with them, creating a sub-species of half-ape, half-eternals, which is about as bad a crime as you can get in the galaxy and brings the Law crashing down on them. Exit evil Eternals, and enter the galactic authorities, who place the planet under edict, putting it out of bounds except for documentary makers, who follow the doings of the half-breeds for immersive movie channels, which bored Eternals across the universe follow obsessively.

No, Wolfgang thought, looking around, the only relevant movie was the one still running here in this room. And the suspense was over how many junkies would end up OD'd or in a perpetual vegetative state. From the twisted position of many of the bodies, blood would have stopped circulating to their extremities, and limbs might have to be amputated. Was this the opening sequence of a court medical drama, highlighting concerns over what the new generation of designer drugs was doing to young people? The evidence debated by expert witnesses, sexual tension provided by an attractive blonde barrister who once slept with the prosecutor, who thinks he hates her but is lying to himself. If so, it needed a dramatic ending to make up for the depressing storyline. Was Supergrass waiting for him to leave before swooping down from his perch to give them parrot disease, so later they'd wake up on the mortician's slab with their eyes pecked out, spouting inane phrases they would repeat for the rest of their lives?

Of one thing Wolfgang was sure, the effects of the acid had worn off, for despite the dim lighting of the room, everything was in prismatic focus. Kicking aside the insensible bodies of heavy drug users he now loathed with every fibre of his being, and cursing the changed times, so different from happier days when he last tripped, he made for the door, closing it behind him without so much as a backwards glance.

The sun was cresting the far ridge when Wolfgang stepped out of the castle's portico and took his first hit of the morning. Snorting cool country air into his nostrils, redolent of moorland flowers, the effect far superior to cocaine, he considered. He looked up at the enclosing hills and the purple heather still in bloom, so late this year, he thought. A sign of hope. Why not.

Lowering his eyes, he noticed Saxon disconsolately kicking a heel against an upturned water barrel, picking his teeth with a 4" nail.

'You slovenly git!' Wolfgang roared, getting into his stride, rapidly crossing the forecourt. 'Back-sliding again? Well I've a job for you. Petrol! I want to see a can and a rubber tube, pronto! You're to syphon every last drop from that heap of tin shit over there.' Swivelling on oiled hips, he pointed commandingly like an admiral of the fleet at a buccaneer's BMW frigate, holed below the waterline, lying dismasted on a reef.

Then, when Saxon stayed rooted to the spot, still saluting idiotically, Wolfgang roared again, 'Jump to it, man, at the bloody double!'

Ever the show-off in the gymnastic dept, diving onto his hands, Saxon cartwheeled away over the lawn, the man mountain spinning in the direction of the shed at the back of the castle.

A shower of small stones heralded Za-Za's sudden appearance as she clambered down a drainpipe from the battlements, kicking aside the thick ivy as she descended, dropping the last few feet to land in a crouch by Wolfgang.

'Did you see him?'

'See who?' Wolfgang asked as she stood up, more interested in what was revealed in rips in her clothing, although the best bits were concealed by daubs of mud, delicately placed.

'Skull, who else? He's only been banging away at me!'

Wolfgang's leer broadened into a grin. 'I'm sure he has, *dearest*. Can I call you that?'

Shaking her head, her eyes suddenly brimming with tears, she snapped, 'Don't get smart, Wolfgang! And especially don't laugh! I've been beaten, look.' She indicated several grazes. 'There, there and there.' Bending her head, she pulled back her hair, exposing an ear.

Was she an actress starring in the movie?

'Wolfie,' she said, sternly, 'pay attention! Do you see the scorch mark from where he shot at me at close range?' Straightening up, she reached into her denim shirt and pulled out a little book from between snowy breasts, plump as Christmas puddings, its slim blue cover embossed with a double headed eagle in gold. 'But I got my damned passport!'

An animal roar redirected Wolfgang from the riddle of the double headed imperitor eagle and what it was doing on a US passport in her cleavage. It was Saxon, making sure both were watching as he wrenched off the BMW's locking petrol cap, tossed it back over his shoulder to join a battered boot lid and a distributor cap in a topiary bush. Smiling cheerily, the man mountain started forcing an overlarge hose into the petrol tank.

'I don't believe it,' Za-Za giggled, 'I've heard of cows and sheep, but no one told me the local yokels fuck cars as well.'

'Shh.' Wolfgang pointed. He had just noticed a bicycle leaning against the last remaining upright section of the trellis fence. 'Come on. Let's go on this, forget my car, I'll fill it up later.'

'Oi, that's ma bike,' Saxon yelled, as Wolfgang clambered aboard, positioning his butt between Za-Za's outsize hands gripping the handle bars.

'Don't worry,' he called back, 'I'll buy you three fish suppers at the chippie in Snaresburgh for the hire of it later.'

'Ocht well I suppose that's alright then...' Saxon turned little boy lost, his voice notching up an octave. 'B.. b.. but whit'll I dae with a' this petral?'

Careful not to overbalance the bicycle as Za-Za provided forward motion on the pedals, Wolfgang twisted around. 'Burn the fucking castle,' he shouted back, 'and start with that garbage can next to Menace's Range Rover.'

Reaching relative safety and holding open the forest gate as Za-Za wheeled the bike through, Wolfgang looked back the way they had come. Over the trees, flames were licking the windows of one of the apartments in the towers. Soon the castle would be ablaze, and hopefully with it the vermin. Mission accomplished, he told himself, even though, when they'd set off the night before, that had not been the objective. Still, he had drawn a line, as Bungalow Bill had advised, had done his bit for the greater good, and it was a job well done.

Happier than he had been in a long, long time, sitting on the handlebars, his hairy legs dangling either side of the front wheel, Wolfgang was content to take in the view as Za-Za pedalled past Loch Duich. Mist plumes arose from its mysterious waters, a squadron of swans splashing down by the reed beds, a plover flying up from a copse of gnarled trees in a green field on the steep east side of Haggard Hill, reflected upside-down in the unfathomable deeps of the bottomless loch, its summit golden in the rays of the dawning sun.

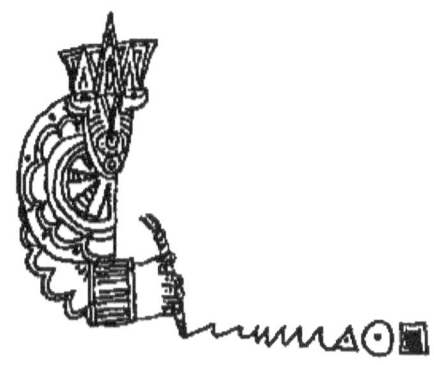

END

The erstwhile Laird was running a coffee shop, 'Strictly half an hour,' his mate promised as he left him in charge of 'Caffeinated Contentment™'. Empty then, the place was now filling up with regulars desperate for their early morning fix. As a barista, Wolfgang was a complete failure, even though he was giving his all. He knew the general terms, beyond the basic black & white and instant of his parents, but what the difference was between a cappuccino *wet* and *dry* he hadn't the remotest idea? Then there were the new expresso subdivisions. So far, he had been asked for a *lungo, a quad* and a *no fun,* and he suspected there would be a lot more. Likewise, Americano, which now he learned could be *double tall, doppio, flat white, half-cut, skinny, half and half* and *with legs.* And that wasn't even including the confusingly named muffins, glowing like radioactive space debris in the glass counter display. So hazardous, apparently, a hairnet and protective gloves were de rigueur, and special steel tongs required to dole them out – never mind the *honey buns, stroop waffles, salt donuts, jam beignets, raspberry croissants, almond biscotti* and *strüdel poodles,* in a separate compartment, dispensed with sterilised pincers. Ice cream had similar precautions, and was served in scalloped dollops, which looked quite small to his eyes, for all the portions were described as *super-sized.* There was an electronic till with a display with luminous little pictures of the above that responded to his finger. Everyone had plastic cards instead of cash, or black devices they waved at the till which somehow charged for their order. What the fuck? He was only doglegging it in Wales, following a forking path traced on his 4d map reader, on-route to meet up with his Inuit amanuensis, and resume dictating his novel, but instead he was running a coffee shop.

5 years refurbishing a castle in the remote wilds of the Kingdom and the World had clearly moved on. Who were these people? His last time in this hill town they were either scrawny sheep farmers subsidized by the RU, or malnourished hippies hiding away from the apocalypse subsisting on benefits and beans, not these branded types, sporting soft clothing bearing the slogans of organizations, nations and penal regimes Wolfgang had never heard of, with wires dangling from white buds in their ears. Neither were there any ashtrays, or indeed any smokers unless he counted the two puffing away outside. It was a puzzle. What was this *lifestyle*, so prominently featured on the glossy cover of the 'Caffeinated Contentment™' brand magazines scattered about? Exactly how did that differ from a life? And what were those devices they were intently tapping, collectively sounding like an insect colony? Were they beaming electronic messages, invisibly through the air? Perhaps not so invisibly, Wolfgang reconsidered, out the corner of his eye catching a glimpse of zipping trails shimmering in the smoke free Welsh air, reminding him of the fox fire he would sometimes see coursing the strings, late at night working on his map back at the castle. Only when he squinted, these luminous strings, though faint, were actually evident in day light, and seemed to be converging on the radio mast on the hill top, framed in the window of the café.

Amazing the changes, he shuddered, trying not to focus on the busy lines of data crossing the room, some perhaps even streaming through his innards, at that moment. To distract himself from what wondering which vital organ the electronic messages might be messing with, he turned his attention back to the customers, lounging on their sofas like snooty Lords and Ladies in a select club for the Gentry or perched on stools hunched at the high tables, which anyway hardly merited the term, being more like flat-backed cockroaches on attenuated legs reflected in the deep gloss of the specially imported African lignum vitae floorboards which showed up every spec of dirt and squashed jam muffin under the cockroach tables. That all being part of the style of the so-called design ethic of Caffeinated Contentment™, as the manager, a former employee at the castle had explained, before running out of the door to answer a 'call', which Wolfgang suspected was not one of nature brought on by his double tall skinny mocha, for he had noticed there was a toilet in the back of the coffee shop, (for *both* sexes!!) but rather was a telephone call on his mate's black device, which had chimed exactly like Big Ben striking the hour before he left so hurriedly. It was almost as disconcerting as hearing the cracked bell of the Clock Tower, back at the Castle, which was missing its clapper, portentously tolling as he drove out of the gates, after signing the pre-divorce agreement negotiated by Jaws, his lawyer, on whom he was now dependent on funds. Crossing the new Scappa Flo Bridge, and safely through the border on the Scottish side, reduced to driving an underpowered second hand banger which he had decided to dump in Wales.

Fortunately however, a couple of nice regulars – girls actually, who disconcertingly referred to themselves as 'guys', had taken pity on Wolfgang, and were helping out behind the counter making the intricacies of the expresso machine look easy, which had not been the case when Wolfgang had hardly been able to see the first customers for gusts of steam, as he pulled at the levers like a demented church organist playing a Bach fugue to a congregation of the damned. As it was the mid-morning rush of caffeine heads from new businesses which, since Wolfgang's last visit, had popped up like hallucinations brought on by magic mushrooms in the formerly boarded shops of the high street, selling windsurfing gear, scented soaps, gastronomic consumables – craft cheese, leek beer and such like, queuing for coffee *to go*, (another new term on Wolfgang) was snaking out the door, (opened by depressing a pad at the side?) where there seemed to be some sort of disturbance with the smokers.

Wolfgang felt a nudge on his arm from Rachel, – one of the girl/guys, who he now understood he was supposed to think of as his co-worker.

'I think you better go help old Nick.' She pointed a star speckled fingernail, at the door, 'that's him just outside. He's always complaining about something,' she shrugged, smiling sweetly. 'But it takes all kinds, dunnit.'

'Can I help you sir,' Wolfgang said, smiling insincerely down at the lanky man folded into the electric assisted wheelchair, who appeared to be a recent convert to the new order sweeping rural Wales, his greying hair pulled back in a lank pony tail, hanging over the astrakhan collar of his smart tweed jacket, which was unbuttoned and clearly a new purchase, unlike his worn yellow waistcoat, stained green corduroy trousers, and scuffed brown brogues, the laces undone on one shoe.

'About time!' he snarled, looking up. 'Can't your café fiend people do something about that bloody ramp.'

'What's wrong with it?' Wolfgang enquired with genuine curiosity, since he associated shop doorways with steps, and wanted to know more.

'Too steep for the servos of my new e-zippy,' the man said, tapping a gloved driving hand to the battery of his sleek electric wheel chair, which appeared to have been designed in a wind tunnel. 'This disabled access is borderline illegal.'

'Sorry to hear that Sir. Assuredly, I will pass your complaint on to the management,' Wolfgang said insincerely, while wondering how a perfectly functional doorway could, at the same time, be borderline disabled *and* illegal, as he smoothly steered the wheelchair past the queue.

'Stop here!' The man ordered abruptly, waving towards the toilet area at the back of the shop. 'Park the e-zippy there. When you are ready, I'll have a half and half mocha and organic Alvera sweetener, with a buttered malted toasty, crème cheese and a slice of lime on the side. I'll be in my usual place,' he pointed to a sagging yellow sofa, which was unoccupied.

'But won't you need your wheel chair? Wolfgang asked, restraining an urge to stuff the grumpy old fart back down into his seat, as he rose from it.

'In case you were wondering, I am not disabled,' the man, who was surprisingly tall, said drawing himself up haughtily, and looking down his flute of a nose at Wolfgang, 'Just vertically challenged, that's all.'

Yes, it was a rude awakening to a very changed world out-with the Kingdom, Wolfgang had in the heartlands in Wales, but a good preparation for his arrival in the big city where his amanuensis impatiently awaited him. The castle, and the moonshine of a buccaneering past, fading in the mists of a Kingdom that time forgot, as the bright colours bled out on the tapestry that Brünhida wove after their marriage, and the shooting star which was supposed to represent him, plunged to earth, before emerging on the far side of the horizon into the brash light of this brand-new day.

SESSION #1

Wolfgang resumed his surveillance of his amanuensis. Behind his new laptop computer, with the double head eagle icon on its raised lid, glowing evilly, she was filing her nails again. By rights, surely by now they should be stumps. Long even strokes, back forth, back forth, it was endless. Christ it was hypnotic. Rasp, rasp. Like a woodman's saw, and about as long.

Where was he? French windows half open onto a small curved balcony, browning leaves falling from the autumnal trees in the street outside. Below the Victorian scrollwork of the balcony's rusting balustrade, the red roof of a double decker bus going past. London then ...

More novels by Will Lorimer
Published by Inkistan.com

INKISTAN
.COM

TRANSEND
Before the Fall

As the Man said, 'It's our job to ensure the END has a time-table ...
Events must be controlled. We can't just bow down to the inevitable!'
The clock is ticking. Preparations are complete. Moun-tain refuges
have been prepared for those with sufficient funds.

After the Fall -

There's the CEO's billionaires, and Politicians living extended
lives under the Mountain, whose status has been reduced to that
of mere numbers.

There's the Punk saboteur, and her orange fireball sidekick,
causing mayhem under the Mountain.

There's the fattest girl in the world who one day will be queen.

There's No. 1 and No. 3 in lockdown in a safe room, wondering
what's going in the corridors beyond.

There's the phosphorescent dust thick in the air, which gets
into everything, even miles underground.

There's the sclerotic eye which wanders the sky and beams
down pestilence on the land below.

There's Bonaparte, only he's black – in charge of the Consensus, who thinks he rules the world.

There's the war between the Consensus, and the Trans-hu-
man rebels, as an even more precipitous Fall, looms.

ASIN: 1911289543 – (paperback) ASIN: B00WPV0E6M (KINDLE)

TRANS END

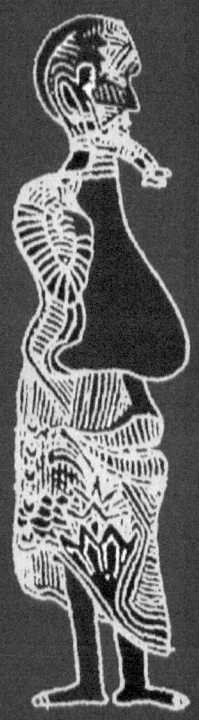

WILL LORIMER

ON THE RUN IN DREAMTIME

(two editions, one illustrated)

An intensive course in enlightenment delivered by Lobo, a tricky Tibetan on a mission to rid the world of dirt, who believes that Frankie is the 'Chosen One'. A pity then that the Chosen One should turn out to be a foul mouthed, none too clean Scotsman. However, Lobo is nothing if not determined.

Together they blaze an unstoppable trail across an unsuspecting Australia, in a pristine white falcon pick-up. From the dives of Kings Cross Sydney, to the wild wastes of flying doctor country, they connive, conspire, and con their way in and out of trouble, in scenarios created by Lobo, intended to demonstrate the secret teachings of his secret Yogic master in a Himalayan cave.

Subjecting his hapless Scottish apprentice, to cruel humiliations, and sleep deprivation, Lobo attempts to cleanse Frankie of his dirty ways in a fast moving comedy of errors that will have you laughing your socks off, page after page, in this classic of road literature.

The story is illustrated by drawings from the Author's travel journal of a round OZ road trip, back in the day.

The Audio Book
On the Run in Dreamtime
- Incomparably narrated by the author -

Browse ⌄   Audible Blog   Free Audiobook   Free Audible Original Podcasts

The AWESOME
HeadfuX

Will Lorimer

Spanning worlds, realities, genres and possibilities, this counter factual novel begs the question – *what if* our reality is faux, all history bunkum, and the mind boggling conspiracy outlined within its pages, true? What if our culture is just an aggregation of stories recorded in the Book of Eternity? *What if* all the great scientists and savants are mere story tellers? *What if* this isn't a novel at all, but instead is the factual account of a nerve-racking tour of the multiverse, by way describing where we come from and are headed. -

KINDLE: ASIN: B00WPV0E6M - **Paperback.** – ASIN: 0956957765

the Last of the Lutchens

THE ILLUSTRATED EDITION

Will Lorimer

(two editions, one illustrated)

Britain over the last hundred years, through the eyes of an An-glo-Scots family of dubious lineage, featuring the illusions and obsessions of three generations of the Lutchens, woven together in a genealogical tree rooted in a Scotland which we only thought we knew. Starting in the swinging sixties as the Beatles' first single tops the charts and the Cuban Crisis looms, the narrative tracks back through two world wars to uncover a skeleton in the family closet, before proceeding full circle, to when a national crisis threatens to break-up the disunited family. Will the Lutchens go their separate ways, or patch up their differences? Everything hangs in the balance for the family, and also the British nation state.

ASIN: B005F7TBEE (KINDLE) ASIN: B00MI574LS (KINDLE)

THE ESCAPE FROM MICTLÁN TRILOGY
- An Overview -
by Alejandro Ehrenberg

It was a secret from his amnesic past that even his NY analyst couldn't decipher, which meant he had to go to Mexico in search of answers, specifically to a ghost town in the bandit-infested Sierra Madre, where his mother was waiting for him at the only hotel in town.

Deep in the Sierra Madre, behind a tunnel carved through the top of a mountain, one of the five that encircled the place like the fingers of a hand, is the strangest ghost town in Mexico. There is a hotel, run by a serial killer, and just across the street, a cantina, run by a drug cartel banker.

The town was founded in 1495, when a band of conquerors who, after the fall of Tenochtitlán, had been hunting the last Aztec eagle warriors in the mountains, found silver in the ashes of the previous night's fire. They were thirteen conquerors, whose descendants ruled the town for four hundred years, the richest in Mexico at the time, with a treasury, a mint, even an opera and of course a cathedral, until Pancho Villa and his North Division took the town in 1914 and shot the descendants of the conquerors, who took the location of the secret treasure to the grave.

After the Revolution, bands of adventurers from the four corners, lured by the legend of the Treasure of the Sierra Madre (some said there were thirteen treasures), dynamited most of the buildings of the medieval town — but of the treasure, or treasures, nothing was ever known. The Nahuas of the remote mountains think that it will never be known, as it is the property of the Lord of Death, king of Mictlán, and whoever discovers its location will be taken to one of the nine levels of the vast kingdom, which lies under the buried silver mines. in the mountains. This is the story of a search for answers, among which is what happened to a disgraced bishop, a damned enormously rich Kabbalist, who left for Mictlán with the secret of the treasures, where his prodigal bastard son has to go, if it is that he wants to decipher the enigmas of his amnesic past.

VOLUME 1

(Copiously illustrated by the Author, from his time researching the story in the peyote badlands of Northern Mexico.)

A prodigal bastard searching the remote Sierra Madre for the last whereabouts of his late father, tracks down the philandering Bishops's former housekeeper, his mother who he suspects of being a serial killer, managing the only hotel in the *town with no name,* where nothing is as it seems, every day is the Day of the Dead, and the cathedral bells toll 13 at midnight. Even the Police chief has fled following the discovery of a mass grave under the bandstand in the main square, and the only safe place is the local cantina, where the barman is the narco-cartel banker.

KINDLE- ASIN: B08DXX9WF4 PAPERBACK - **ASIN: 183813820X**

VOLUME 2

WILL LORIMER

ESCAPE FROM MICTLÁN

A prodigal bastard's search for his father continues, from the Town with No Name, over the last unmapped mountain range in Mexico, to Narco HQ. Warmly welcomed by an old compadre, their reunion, however, is cruelly short when the evil Baron's black helicopters, swoop down on the hidden canyon and the *narco-revolucinarios.* Pursued into caverns, a *Generalissimo* disgraced, fleeing battle – cornered, he plunges into a subterranean torrent and is swept away … Eventually, to Mictlán, and his new employment under the terms of his contract with the presiding demon, as the Ferryman, on the Black River. Where it's true, dead men tell strange tales, and pay for the privilege, in gold coin to a prodigal bastard, slowly punting the stiffs, shore to shore, to their last resting place in the Wall of Niches on the far side of Perdition - *once upon a time in Mictlán ...*

KINDLE - ASIN: B08FG9JWN7

(The Spanish Language Edition of the 3 volumes
translated by Alejandro Ehrenberg)

el Espíritu que
jamas se entregó

Will Lorimer

ASIN: 1548139157

DOG DAYS IN NEW YORK

A collection of short stories of life in Manhattan in the
early 1980's.
Illustrated by the Author.

Kindle – ASIN: B0883FTFYP -

WILL LORIMER
IS A MULTIMEDIA ARTIST

EVERY PICTURE TELLS A STORY,
AND EVERY POEM IS A PICTURE
IN THIS TRAVELOGUE THROUGH
THE MIND OF THE ARTIST
CHARTING THE ABSURDITIES,
FOLLIES AND DELUSIONS OF OUR
TROUBLED TIMES.

"TOTALLY UNIQUE ... VASTLY ENTERTAINING..."
MARTIN BEZANT

WHO'S ART #1

WILL LORIMER

WHO'S ART?

PICTURE POEMS #1

1980-2020

WILL LORIMER

MEET   THE
AUTHOR

Will Lorimer is a multimedia artist. He attended the
Scottish School of Hard Knocks and graduated with a PHD
in survival strategies.

To find out more about his Art
visit **Inkistan.com**

Take a trip to Inkistan, and
discover the wonderful world of
Will's multi-media Art.

www.ingramcontent.com/pod-product-compliance
Lightning Source LLC
Chambersburg PA
CBHW030259130626
46549CB00002B/608